Also by Richard Bach

Stranger to the Ground

Biplane

Nothing by Chance

Jonathan Livingston Seagull

A Gift of Wings

Illusions

There's No Such Place as Far Away

The Bridge Across Forever

One

Running from Safety

Out of My Mind

Rescue Ferrets at Sea

RICHARD BACH

THE FERRET CHRONICLES

Illustrated by the Author

Ferret House Press

Air Ferrets Aloft

SCRIBNER
NEW YORK LONDON TORONTO SYDNEY SINGAPORE

SCRIBNER
1230 Avenue of the Americas
New York, NY 10020

This book is a work of fiction. Names, characters, places, and incidents either are products of the author's imagination or are used fictitiously. Any resemblance to actual events or locales or persons, living or dead, is entirely coincidental.

For information regarding special discounts for bulk purchases, please contact Simon & Schuster Special Sales at 1-800-456-6798 or business@simonandschuster.com

Designed by Carla J. Stanley
Text set in Fry's Baskerville

Manufactured in the United States of America

1 3 5 7 9 10 8 6 4 2

Library of Congress Cataloging-in-Publication Data

Bach, Richard.
Air ferrets aloft/Richard Bach.
p. cm.—(The ferret chronicles)
1. Ferrets—Fiction. I. Title.

PS3552.A255 A75 2002
813'.54—dc21
2002017621

ISBN 0–7432–2753–0

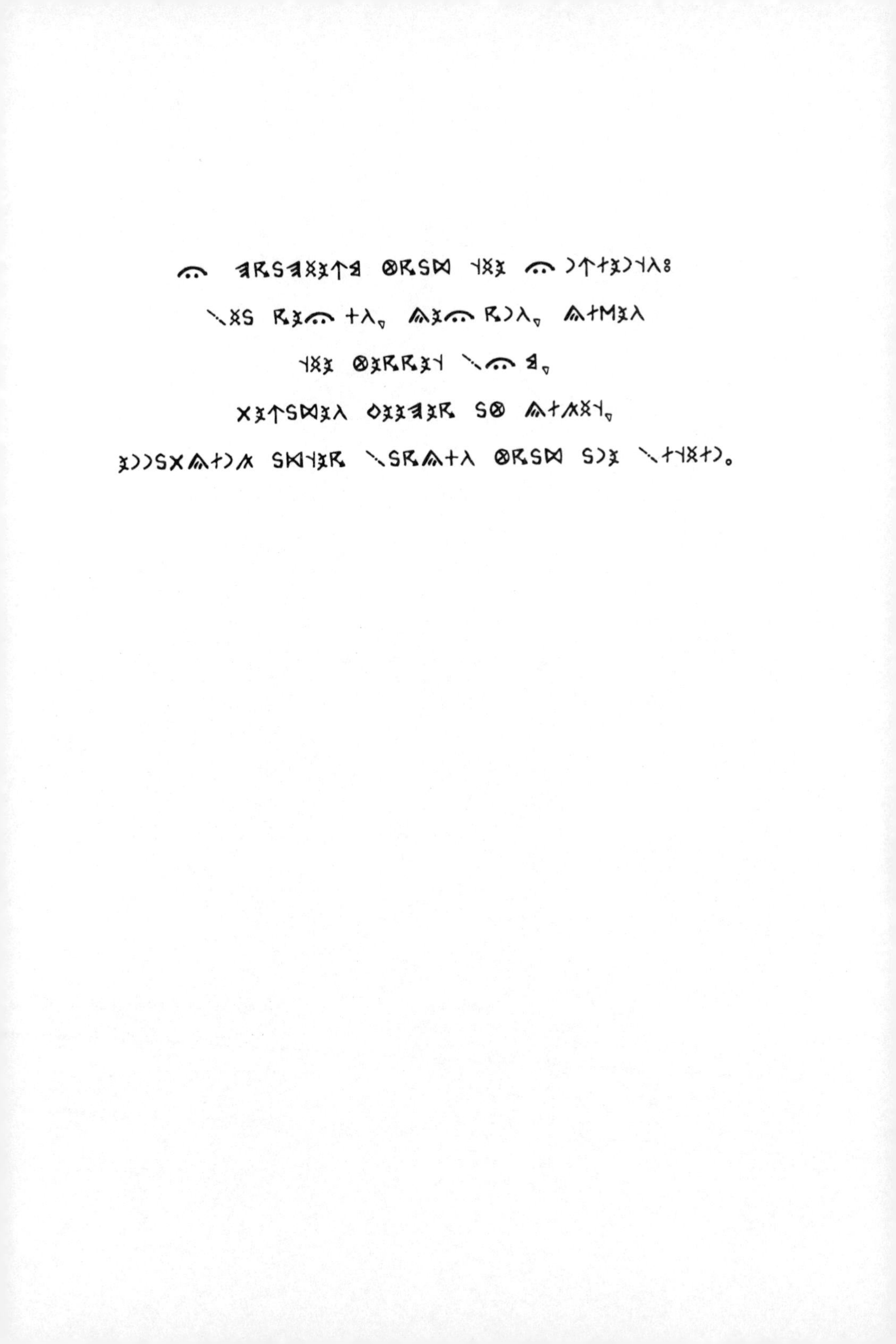

Air Ferrets Aloft

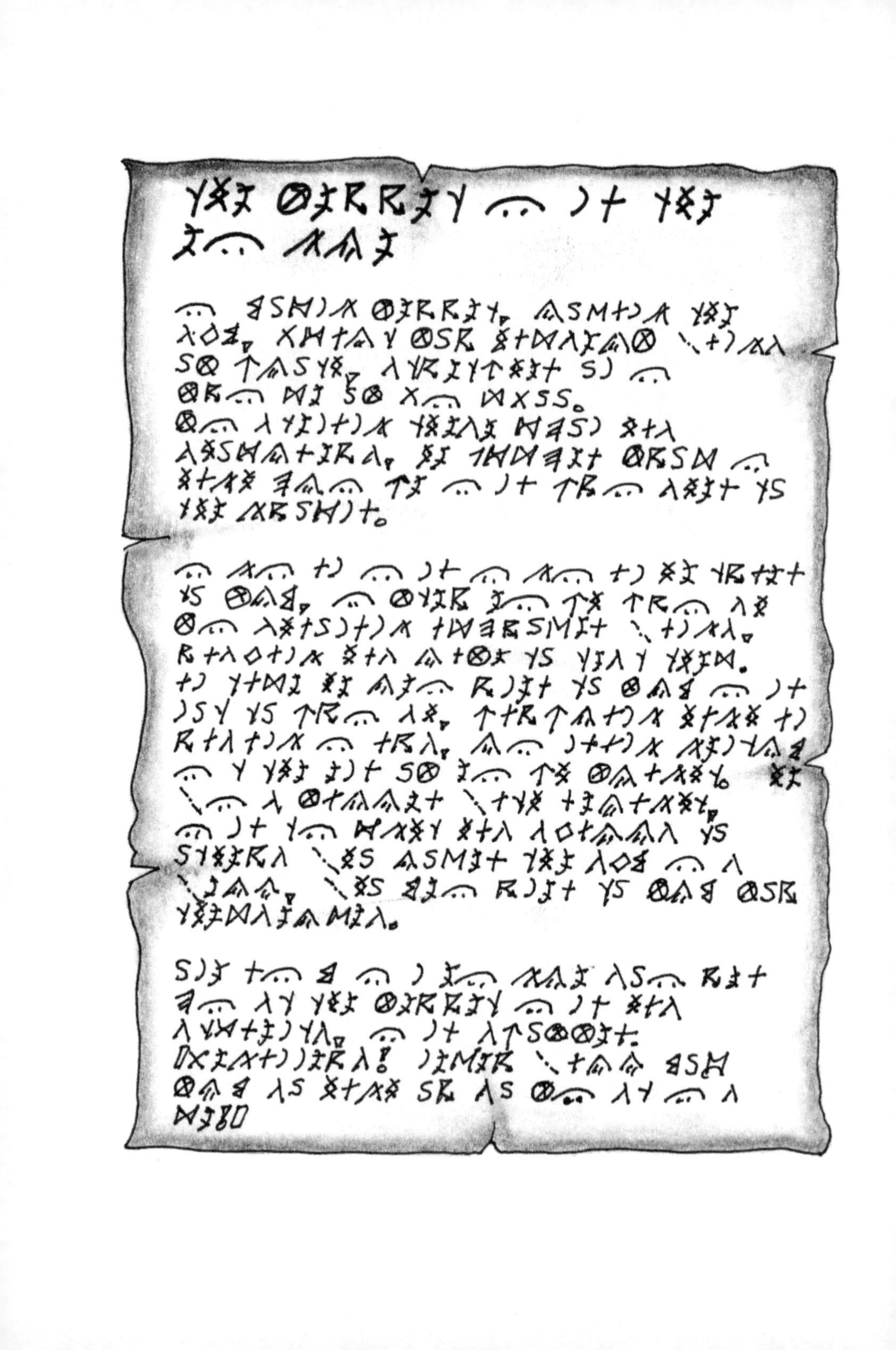

The Ferret and the Eagle

A young ferret, loving the sky, built for himself wings of cloth, stretched on a frame of bamboo. Fastening these upon his shoulders, he jumped from a high place and crashed to the ground.

Again and again he tried to fly, after each crash fashioning improved wings, risking his life to test them. In time he learned to fly and not to crash, circling high in rising airs, landing gently at the end of each flight. He was filled with delight, and taught his skills to others who loved the sky as well, who yearned to fly for themselves.

One day an eagle soared past the ferret and his students, and scoffed. "Beginners! Never will you fly so high or so fast as me!"

Hearing this, the students were discouraged, for it seemed to them that what the eagle said was true, that a ferret's place was on the ground.

"Be not dismayed by the eagle's words," their teacher told them, "for the mark of true flight is not our altitude but our attitude, not our speed but our joy in the paths we find above the earth."

The students listened, welcomed his truth to be their own. Aloft again, they treasured their adventures and skills and discoveries as never they had before, and passed along to younger ferrets the wisdom they learned from the sky.

We are led, when we share our loves, to an enchanted life of inner happiness, which unsharing others cannot know.

—Antonius Ferret, *Fables*

CHAPTER 1

POMPOM FERRET sat in the pilot's seat, one small paw on the engine throttles, surrounded by panels of flight instruments, levers and gages, knobs and switches.

The kit turned her powder-color mask upward, puzzled. "But what makes it fly, sir?"

Gold-stripe scarf tied neatly at his throat, captain's hat brushed and polished, Strobe Ferret was chief pilot for MusTelCo, the largest ferret corporation in the world. He had heard the question a thousand times at airshows, time and again from the young animals who came to tour the FerrJet's flight deck.

"Magic!" he said. "There, out the window, see the wing—can you see the curve on top of the wing?"

The little face turned, solemn black eyes, nodded at seamless metal, white and royal blue. Outside, a gentle crowd, ferrets of every age strolling down rows of aircraft at the Air Expo, touching wings, peering through windshields, asking questions, telling stories of flight. Pompom looked for the magic.

"When we move a wing through the air, that simple curve, it pushes air down. When we move it fast, it pushes a lot of air down. And when it pushes air down, what happens to a wing?"

Pompom turned from the sight, eyes sparkling at the captain, sudden understanding. "It goes up!"

"Magic," he said, "and it can be you, making it happen someday." He grinned at her. "Pretend we're in the air. Now show me how we make the airplane climb."

The kit reached a paw, unsure, touched the control wheel.

"That's it," said Strobe. "Ease the wheel back and we go up; forward, and we go down. Turn it left," he asked, "and . . . ?"

Floating behind them on the flight deck, at the edge of the dimension between two worlds, hovered a tiny golden helicopter, a single angel ferret fairy at the controls.

From his soap-bubble cockpit, the ghost pilot paused, warmed by the scene. Then Tech Angel Gnat turned back to his work. So long had it been since he was mortal that he had forgotten how it felt to be locked in a body reluctant to turn invisible or to pass through walls and doors.

Mortalhood is a fine state to visit, he thought, the *dook-dook-dook* of his rotor blades echoing as the helicopter slipped inside the FerrJet's cabin-pressure system, but it's no place to call home.

Gnat's passion on earth had been flight, and his death had changed nothing. Flight was his passion still.

First-rate maintenance, he frowned, inspecting the joints and seals of the system under his helicopter spotlight, checking screws and bolts and safety wires. Somewhere in this aircraft there has to be a flaw. If not maintenance overlooked, he hoped, then it'll be wear, or a tool left loose in the system, or metal fatigue.

I'll find a weakness, Gnat told himself. It's for his own good. If I have to break it myself, this aircraft will not finish the run that Captain Strobe Ferret has planned to fly tonight.

He reached the outflow valve, inspected it, moved on. Then on strange intuition, he turned back, looked closer. The smallest smile, and he pressed his microphone button, spoke softly on the angel ferret fairy communication frequency.

"Pinecone has the red light," he said. "Pinecone has the red light."

CHAPTER 2

"THERE'S A FERRET in the sky!" From the hillside, gathering berries, the kit pointed. "See, Mom? She's reaching for something. There's her nose. See her paws, stretching up?"

The kit's mother looked heavenward. "It's a beautiful ferret, Tabitha. Let's watch her change, now . . ."

The two stopped, sat on the grass, berry basket between them, facing the tall, sleek cloud. From time to time they'd choose a blueberry, then watch the cloud once more.

After a while: "Isn't it going to melt?"

"It will. Clouds change as they blow along with the wind."

They watched. Other clouds changed, theirs didn't.

"When a ferret cloud keeps its shape, do you know what that means, Tabby?"

"No, Mother."

"They say that when ferret clouds don't swirl and tumble, it means there are angel ferret fairies inside, and the cloud won't float away till their meeting's over."

"Oh . . . ," said the kit. "That's just a story, isn't it?"

"Could be," said her mother. "But isn't it odd, the way your cloud doesn't change?"

"Order!" called Taminder, from the front of the room. "Could we have a little order, please?"

Parked on the cloud outside were a dozen tiny helicopters, the colors of sunrise. Within the glowing whiteness of the briefing room ranged their pilots, ferrets no larger than a pawprint, all chattering and listening at once, none of them to Taminder.

"I'd appreciate a little order!" said the chief angel ferret fairy. He sighed. They were excellent pilots, every one of them, or they wouldn't be here. They were fearless, innovative, resourceful, every one a volunteer . . . just the animals to call upon when destinies needed to meet.

Now this elite task force was more interested in swapping old adventures than hearing about the new one to come.

"Parker Ferret was going to walk by Simoune, he was lost in thought, he was going to pass right by. You can imagine—their guardian angels were going crazy, I was the closest angel ferret fairy, and they said, 'We need help, Pavo, now!' Do you know what I did?"

"You made her sneeze," said Gawaine. "No. You made a butterfly land on her shoulder. That's what I would have done. And Parker saw the butterfly and, instead of walking past, he said, 'How do you do that?' Right?"

"No," said Pavo. "I made her sneeze."

"Oh. Did it work?"

"Of course it worked. But I like your butterfly idea . . ."

"Order, please, angel ferret fairies!"

It didn't go quiet in the briefing room, but the noise dropped a little. Taminder nodded toward the cloud wall, and at once appeared the image of a young ferret, her fur the color of snow, streaked with night. She wore the cap and scarf of a pilot. From the scene, one could hear a muffled thunder of engines.

For a long moment he stood uncaring of the fairies' chatter, watching the image. It had been so long, he thought, she had come so far.

At last he realized that the room was still.

"Thank you," said Taminder. "Her name is Janine, they call her Stormy."

"She's pretty!"

Taminder considered before confirming the comment. He hadn't thought of her beauty before. "Yes, she is a pretty ferret." He cleared his throat. "This is not a practice, gentle fairies, this is a Class Three intervention. Code name: Operation Midnight Snack."

There was a murmur in the room, pilots wrote the words on their kneeboards.

"The others *failed?*"

"Every one."

Had a snowflake fallen upon the cloud floor, it would have been heard by all. What they heard instead was the *dook-dook-dook-dook-dook* of tiny rotor blades, outside.

The sound faded and an angel ferret fairy entered, a newcomer, not long ago a mortal himself.

"Sorry I'm late."

"Welcome to our meeting, Baxter," said Taminder.

"Wrong cloud," the angel muttered, seating himself with the other pilots upon the misty floor.

"Operation Midnight Snack," the chief fairy repeated, for Baxter's benefit. "Her name is Stormy."

An image appeared alongside the first, another aviator, older than the female, his fur the color of walnut. Like her, he was seated at the controls of an airplane.

"This is Strobe," said Taminder. "I must tell you first of all that these are determined mortals."

He watched the pictures, then turned and faced the angel ferret fairy pilots. "Strobe and Stormy have high ideals, of course; we all do. But these two are particularly rigorous in their devotion to the mission—one might say stubborn, one might say headstrong, one might say inflexible."

The pilots shifted uneasily. More than one had ignored their own destiny's subtle hints.

Baxter, just arrived from Angel Ferret Fairy School, was unaffected. What happens, happens, he thought. There's no such thing as a big deal. Everything, always, works out for the best.

"They must meet," said Taminder.

The newcomer raised his paw.

"Yes, Baxter."

"Aren't there alternate worlds, sir? So even if Stormy and Strobe don't meet in this one, they will in . . . ?"

"Of course there are alternate worlds," said Taminder. It was a fair question for someone new to ask. "But our highest sense of right is to express the most possible love in this world, and to help others do so. Alternate worlds can handle their affairs as they wish."

Baxter nodded, satisfied, turned back to the images. Strobe was a handsome animal, one that he hadn't met. There was something about Stormy, however, that was intensely familiar. He couldn't place her. A good memory for faces, he'd had that on earth, he had it now. He knew that look, but he couldn't place her at all.

"Their guardian angels have asked us to help," said Taminder. "Strobe and Stormy Ferret, if they meet, there will be . . . they'll change the world for a lot of animals. But this is the last chance, on our time line, to make it happen." He paused, reached for his light-pointer. "If I may have the chart, please."

An aeronautical chart flashed on the wall of cloud. Taminder lifted the pointer and a glowing red arrow slid along the colored airways.

"Stormy will be heading south, here, down airway Victor Two-Three. She's a pilot for Air Ferrets, flying an FDC-4 out of Seattle for Salinas."

A murmur once again, this time glad recognition. The four-engine Ferret DC-4 is a favorite cargo plane. A number of the fairies present had flown the aircraft when they were mortals, and once one has flown an honest lovely airplane, one never forgets.

The pointer moved. "Northbound up Victor Two-Three will come Strobe."

The fairies leaned forward, watching the plot thicken, beginning to see their part in the drama to come.

"He's MusTelCo's chief pilot. That's Stilton Ferret's company, of course. He'd trust Strobe with his life. They're old friends. Strobe's the pilot in command wherever Stilton flies. There's no finer aviator alive."

The fairies nodded, keen minds flying ahead, addressing the challenge. This is no kits' play, it's a Class III intervention.

"Tonight, Strobe will be flying alone, bringing the FerrJet back to Medford from the Air Expo in Los Angeles. More than one kit's decided to become a pilot, meeting Strobe at an airshow."

A paw raised.

"Bailey?" said the chief fairy.

"All due respect, sir. But no way they're going to meet . . ."

". . . because the FerrJet's up at altitude and Stormy's flying low?"

"Yes, sir."

It was an obvious question. "We have had one bit of luck. Tech Angel Gnat's started a chain."

The ferret fairies turned to each other, pleased with the news.

"First link," said Taminder. "Gnat found metal fatigue, a weak spring in the FerrJet's cabin-pressure system. He bent it a little, and just after takeoff, the spring's going to fail. That's going to drive the cabin-pressure outlet valve full open."

"Well done," the fairies murmured. "Good job, Gnat . . ."

"Our second link is Strobe himself. There was so much demand for oxygen by the other jets at the show that he stood back, let the other pilots have it instead of refilling his own supply. With cabin pressure, who needs oxygen?"

The fairies smiled.

"Without cabin pressure, though, and without oxygen," their chief continued, "Captain Strobe Ferret . . ."

". . . will have to fly at low altitude," said the fairies together.

Taminder nodded.

A question from the back of the room: "The weather?"

"Unfortunately," said Taminder, "the weather's fine."

Baxter raised his paw. "Excuse me . . ."

The leader waited.

"This Stormy, sir. I've never seen her, but I know her face. It's hard to explain but I . . . do you follow me?"

The chief nodded. "Stormy's a Columbine."

The pilot looked blank.

"She's from Columbine Pod. Columbine Family," said Taminder. "Have you not been told about true families?"

"Why, yes, sir, I have."

"Stormy's a Columbine, same as, I believe . . . same as your grandkit, Willow."

The fairy's jaw dropped. Stormy's from Willow's family? Of course! The same flash in her eyes, that same learn-or-die look that had made Baxter shower the kit with toys and puzzles, such a short while ago. Now she grieved for her grampa; he couldn't get through to her that he was all right.

". . . part of the plan," the chief was saying. "If we make this happen, if Stormy meets Strobe, then later she'll meet Willow, when Willow's a Teacher. They're Columbines, it's rare, and the creative connection between them is going to . . ."

"My little Willow's going to be a *Teacher?*"

"Didn't you know?"

"And Stormy will change her life?"

Taminder shrugged. "Of course. Not just Willow's life, if Stormy meets Strobe, but thousands of other . . ."

Baxter rose to his paws as though he would take over the meeting. "Well, if the problem's the weather, can't we do something to change it?"

Taminder frowned. "Great souls share great ideas, Baxter. Perhaps you could take your seat?"

The leader turned back to the chart. "Do we agree? Redding airport is here, nearly on the airway, just south of the Siskiyou Mountains. If they both cancel their flight plans and divert to Redding at the same time, they're sure to meet."

The fairies shook their heads, doubting. Two determined mortal fliers cancel their instrument flight plans and divert to Redding? This was not going to be easy.

"If it were easy, their guardian angels wouldn't need us. We are professionals, gentlefairies. Coincidence is our business."

Taminder's reminder helped; the fluffy room filled with determination.

"Gnat, you've got a way with weather. Do you think you can generate enough turbulence aloft to make Stormy change her mind about flying straight through to Salinas tonight?"

"Over the Siskiyou? With energy from the Shasta Vortex? How do you want me to do it, sir, blindfolded or with four paws and my tail tied? Piece of cake!"

Gnat found this work delicious. He loved behind-the-scenes, the code words of his trade, his special skills with aeronautics, his influence upon the world of mortals.

Taminder did not smile. "Remember how she got her name," he said. "Once she's taken off, Stormy Ferret has never turned back because of rough weather. Never. She doesn't have passengers to worry about, it's just herself and her cargo."

"Siskiyou Mountains are easy for storms, sir. Bad storms."

"Thank you, Gnat. You'll remain Pinecone for this mission?"

"No, sir. Requesting code name Goosebeak."

By the time one becomes chief angel ferret fairy, one has infinite patience. "Thank you, Goosebeak." Taminder dropped the arrow of his pointer south on the chart. "Here's the hard part. We're going to need another storm, over Sacramento. A major storm. We need to catch these two ferrets between, so the only place they *can* divert is Redding."

"There's a May's Diner at Redding," said one of the fairies.

Taminder nodded. There was hardly an airport without a May's Diner for ferret aviators. "I need a team to generate the Sacramento storm."

Silence in the room.

"This will be difficult," said Taminder. "Not much help from nature. Fog is easy over Sacramento. Violent storm is not."

The fairies considered the challenge.

Baxter stood. "I'll do it, sir."

A hint of a smile from the chief angel ferret fairy. "Thank you for offering, Baxter. I'm glad you've got the desire, that's important. But you need the skill to bring this off, and you don't have that, yet."

Gnat raised his paw. "Suggestion, sir?"

"Go ahead, Goosebeak."

"I think I can do Sacramento, sir. I know I can. If I build a storm fast enough over the Sierra, the mountains will block it, force it to pile up west. The only place it can go is right down Victor Two-Three."

As he spoke, he convinced himself. "We can energize from the Tahoe Vortex or the one at Half Dome. Why don't you put Baxter in the Siskiyou, sir, instead of me? His grand-kit's a Columbine, he'll know Stormy's mind before she does herself. Nimble and Prestor can help him cook up a terrifying storm, they can do it easy there. Baxter can tell them just how much is enough, without tearing her air-plane to pieces."

Nimble hadn't been sure enough of his skills to volunteer for a Class III intervention, but now he looked at his partner. Prestor nodded I can if you can.

"We'll do that," said Nimble.

Taminder switched off the light-pointer "Thank you, gentle-fairies. Stormy and Strobe will be in the intervention area two hours after midnight. This is our last chance, or these two will never meet. Esther, I'd like you to be the energy boss, your team can set an axis." He paused, considering. "No. Not an axis, Esther. Set a triangle. We'll use the Shasta Vortex, and Tahoe and Half Dome, in Yosemite."

Near the back of the room, a striking black-sable ferret stood. "All three vortices, sir? That's a good deal of energy . . ."

"We'll need it. We'll need two major storms. Anything less, Stormy's going to fly straight through. Probably Strobe will, too."

"Yes, sir."

"Any questions?" said Taminder.

Silence from the group, but all thought the same: power from Shasta and Tahoe, yes . . . *and Yosemite?*

"Very well. Their angels are counting on us. Start engines at your discretion, gentlefairies. Let's do it right!"

The berries were eaten, most of them, the basket nearly empty.

"The ferret's fading!"

Her mother watched. "Tabitha, honey, you're right!" The tall cloud twisted in slow motion, gradually became a swan, melting away.

"What is it now, Tab?"

"It's a cloud," said the kit, the snowy fur around her mouth turned the color of blueberries. "Does that mean the angel ferret fairies have gone away?"

CHAPTER 3

THE NIGHT, on Victor 23, belongs to the air-cargo pilots.

Round midnight, out of May's Airport Diner, close on the loading docks at Seattle-Tacoma International Airport, the old propeller planes, the twin-engine turboprops and the four-engine cargo liners top off with high-octane and jet fuel.

Before they climb to their flight decks, the pilots, human and ferret alike, check their aircraft landing gear, ailerons and elevators and rudders, wing flaps and beacons and running lights.

Settled in their cockpits, pilots' hands and paws move fuel levers, ignition and starter switches—propeller blades and turbines spin to life in the sounds of flight beginning.

Machines with wings taxi through a maze of blue lights and finally, cleared for takeoff, howl up into the darkness toward Portland and Medford, Salt Lake and Paris, Anchorage and Honolulu and San Francisco and London and Hong Kong.

Midnight-thirty on the dot. A Trans-World Cargo Express wide-body jet, bound for Tokyo, released its brakes and pushed into the night, two hundred tons of fuel and steel and human crew accelerating into the dark, the runway trembling in the crackle and thunder of its engines.

Next in line for takeoff, four miniature radial engines cowled in aluminum, *Air Ferrets* painted crimson and yellow down its side, taxied an FDC-4 transport, wingspan 121 paws, twenty paws from the bottom of its wheels to the tip of its rudder. Its full gross weight was less than a single tire of the humans' monster jet, but in the air traffic system it was not an ounce less important than other aircraft.

On the flight deck within, Captain Janine Ferret reached a snowy paw and touched the flap control lever to *Takeoff*.

"Air Ferret Three-Five," called the tower operator, a specialist ferret working the late shift alongside human traffic controllers, "cleared into position and hold."

The captain pressed the microphone button on her control yoke. "Air Ferret Three-Five, position and hold."

Unimpressed with the size of the TWE transport, at home in the system, Janine Ferret had been flying air cargo for a long time, now. Her bright black eyes, her night-streaked silver fur, her flying scarf the color of gold and lace offered no hint of the skills she'd learned or the life she'd lived in the sky. Only her captain's hat, worn and creased under her headphones, gave a clue.

Under her right paw, engine throttles crept forward and the SkyFreighter taxied onto the runway, its nosewheel coming to a stop on a centerline hot from the fire of the widebody's monster engines.

An easy run tonight, she thought. A little rain this side of Portland, then the weather report promised clear skies all the way to Salinas. Not that it mattered. The weather check was a formality, she'd fly her night missions no matter what the forecast called. It was not so much the cargo that mattered, she knew, but the idea of the cargo, her airline's principle: freight shipped on Air Ferrets will arrive on time.

Behind the flight deck of her transport, secure on pallets tied to the floor of the hold, were fifty containers of cargo—ferret food and bell-balls on their way south.

The tower operator peered at Stormy's airplane through binoculars, called as he watched from the high glass cab. "Air Ferret Three-Five, you're cleared for takeoff, caution wake turbulence the departing aircraft."

"Ferret Three-Five's rolling."

She touched her flight timer and transponder switches, tightened her claws around the four throttles, thrust her paw smoothly forward and released the brakes. So long as she lifted off before the place on the runway where the wide-body became airborne, she'd have no trouble with the giant jet's wake.

Blue flame from the exhaust stacks, a whirling blast of propellers drove the transport down the runway, centerline moving, then blurring below, dropping away. Her airplane flew.

The ferret reached to her right, moved a wheel-shaped lever to the *Up* position, heard the whine and growl of landing gear retracting. Soon three up-and-locked lights glowed red on the instrument panel.

As she reached her paw to the flap-retraction handle, her machine was swallowed in cloud; rain cracked against the windshield, each drop swept away at once in the wind. Before the flaps were up, she had switched her attention to the flight instruments, mechanical windows into gyroscope skies, and relaxed into the routine of weather flying.

"Air Ferret Three-Five," called the tower, "contact Seattle Departure, have a good flight."

"Ferret Three-Five." Though she appreciated the kindness, Stormy wondered why those four extra words. Of course she'd have a good flight—she was in command of the aircraft! But those seconds on the same wish, over and over, add up to a lot of chatter, she thought, no purpose.

She turned a frequency selector and pressed her microphone button. "Hello, Seattle Departure," she said, her voice unhurried. "Ferret Three-Five is through one thousand two hundred paws for five thousand."

She touched the heading hold button on the autopilot, engaged the vertical speed and set the altitude hold to *5*.

The rain snapped on her transport's windshield as it climbed through the weather, not the sound of water as much as a sound of gravel, hard and sharp against the angled glass.

Stormy Ferret loved her work, though it was not the stuff of glamour. She was aloft in the dark because there were ferrets sleeping tonight in Salinas depending on her for their food, kits depending on her for bell-balls in their play, though few would ever know it, few would ever see her aircraft or meet its captain.

"Ferret Three-Five is level at five thousand," she said presently. "Higher anytime."

Alone she flew, cleared through seven thousand and finally leveling at nine thousand paws, settled onto the airway called Victor 23 and into the routine of a long-haul air-cargo pilot.

The rain lashed her airplane. A lone animal high above the ground, her sleek features dim in the red glow of instrument lights, her paws touching this panel or that one, changing radio frequencies from Departure Control to Seattle Center southbound. The temperature outside hovered at freezing; on the windshield the rain clumped now into tiny ice-craters before the wind scoured them away.

So few of us, she thought, so few ferret air-cargo pilots. She sighed. Sometimes she almost wished she could be a normal ferret, snug in some soft hammock, asleep the night through.

"But who would feed us?" she said aloud on her flight deck. "Who would fly food for the ferrets, or bring hammocks and blankets, or toys for the kits?"

It's not an easy job, she thought, but I've been trusted with a mission. There is treasure behind me, fifty containers full. Rain or not, ice or not, it will get through, on time.

Seattle lost in the dark behind her, Portland lost in the dark ahead, her transport broke through the rain, rumbled between lofty canyons of cloud silvered in starlight.

The faithful old SkyFreighter, once so much complex metal and strange systems, had become more familiar than her own battered little automobile. She could no longer tell where her paws stopped and the aircraft began. She felt the wind as though it keened over her own fur. She no longer thought of what she had to do to make the airplane turn and climb, she thought *turn-and-climb* and it happened, metal wings and tail her body in the air.

Sky of ink, stars tiny beacons from heaven, warm breathing of engines . . . the beauty of it took her heart now as it had on her first night flight. An enchanted high land, the sky, a land of secret palaces only fliers could find.

A wall of mist directly ahead, Stormy took one last look at the stars before the SkyFreighter plunged again into the weather. Midnight clouds, wings and propellers and engines and instruments, headings and courses and altitudes in the wild pure arena of the air. She loved it.

From the time she was a kit, Janine Ferret had willed herself into the sky. Hiding in the tall grass not far from her home in Steep River, Idaho, her back against cool earth, she lost herself in the clouds turning overhead, saw herself playing among them.

Asleep in her hammock after bedtime, she dreamed of flying, of grassy hillsides down which she would run, faster and faster, then leap and spread her paws wide to soar upon the wind. So delicious, that melting of her soul into the sky; her dreams were sweet remembering what it is to be free of weight and body both.

It was magic she dreamed, for desires are magic indeed. A spirit that longs to soar, she knew, must by grace and the help of angels find a way to lift into that enchanted blue, and stay.

Her parents were artists, Glinda Ferret the potter and Denver the painter, the two in those days unknown beyond the town limits of Steep River. Stormy's kithood home was a gallery of easels and canvas and colors, clay and glaze and bowls and vases just out of her mother's kiln.

At Janine's room, the sky began. The kit had built models of ferret airplanes, dozens of them: biplanes and seaplanes and gliders and cargo planes, helicopters and trainers and racers, all in miniature. These hung by threads from her ceiling, stood upon her shelves by the books she read about flying.

Her parents would poke paint-spattered noses, clay-speckled whiskers into her doorway, see the newest models hanging, smile at their silver-fur daughter. They had helped her color her room noon-blue, fleecy white on walls and ceiling, luminous stars to shine overhead come dark. "Dear Janine!" they marveled. "Is it true you're going to *fly?*"

They were happy on the ground, they didn't hear the call of the sky, but they watched the young one listening. "Take your time to decide," they told their kit, "but once you know your highest right, run toward it and never look back!"

Stormy had lived that way ever since. Wherever her heart was bound, Mom and Dad would cheer the journey no matter how far it took her from home. How many times she had thanked them for honoring her choices, small ones first, then life-changing ones, till finally they blessed her and let her fly free, into her own destiny.

Each time a freight run took her near Coeur d'Alene, Stormy was off to the house at Steep River to share her

FINAL ASSEMBL
A) Glue floats to wing as
B) Glue engine and pylon to upp
fuselage. Do not attach propeller.
C) Glue left wing, then right wing

adventures, to listen to theirs as the arts of Glinda and Denver Ferret became known, gradually, across the land.

Engulfed in cloud, Stormy pressed a switch labeled *Port-side Ice-Light*. A beam of white shot out from the left fuselage, illuminating wing and engines. Through the beam raced a thousand comets, raindrops and snowflakes, trails of cold fire. The first snowflakes were beginning to freeze on the black-rubber de-ice boots along the wing's leading edge. She touched the switch again and the light went out.

Constantly the ferret rechecked her airplane's flight and engine instruments, while the autopilot held the controls. It would be nearly five hours until she'd fly her approach into Salinas, skating through the weather she knew would be waiting, down between the mountains funneling to the airport.

She reached to her flight bag, opened a small box of ferret food, nibbled absently, her black eyes scanning the instrument panel.

The only thing wrong with cargo flying, she thought, is that it's lonely. A copilot to talk with on the long hauls, that would be pleasant. But when Air Ferrets management had asked its captains if they believed a copilot was necessary for the safety of flight, Stormy had voted no.

Long hours away from home, it's not easy for a commercial pilot to find a mate, and Stormy had not done so. She could not imagine life with a ferret who did not love to fly, himself. So much of her time was aviation. Days off, she flew kits in her own seaplane, inspiring them as she had been inspired by others when she learned to fly. She loved to watch those faces on their first flight, just at the moment of liftoff.

No warning, a jolt of turbulence so sharp it took her breath, slammed her down in her seat, a clash and jangle of bell-balls from the cargo containers behind her. Yellow light glowed on the panel: *Autopilot Disconnect.*

She didn't notice, but at that moment Stormy Ferret had been joined in the dark by three tiny helicopters, the angel ferret fairies Prestor, Nimble and Baxter, the latter flying as close to her window as he dared, striving for a look at the pilot who could one day change his grandkit's life.

So much she didn't see. Far down the airway, a FerrJet aloft, heading north, the captain choosing to fly at a much lower altitude than usual for the failure of his airplane's cabin pressure. Had Stilton Ferret been aboard, Strobe would have returned at once for repair, but tonight he flew alone.

Also unseen, code name Goosebeak and a team of angel ferret fairies tampering with the earth's energy to boil storms for two.

"Stormy, hello!" said Baxter, his mind to hers. "It's important to everybody for you to divert tonight. We need you to land . . ."

"Oh-oh . . ." She saw the disconnect light, moved the autopilot switch to *Off,* then *On* again, pressed *Heading Hold.* Instead of engaging the flight controls and steering the airplane, the autopilot tugged at the control wheel, twisting to the right, and disconnected again.

Stormy Ferret sighed and took the wheel, holding the transport on heading and altitude by paw as it swept over Portland. The windows of her flight deck might as well have been painted black, the pilot alone in a tiny room suspended high midair, only her instruments to tell up from down, left from right, and those submerged in a pool of dim red cockpit light.

She pulled and reset the autopilot circuit breaker, adjusted trim wheels to be certain the machine was flying without pressures on the flight controls, then one more time tried the autopilot switch. One more time the airplane lurched to the right before the system shut itself off.

Ferret transports have backup communication and navigation radios, of course, and fuel cross-feed, should an engine fail. They do not have standby autopilots, however, and though her workload increases when the system fails, the captain is expected to control the airplane the old-fashioned way, by paw.

She shifted her seat forward a notch and continued her instrument scan, coaxing the transport left when it was thrown right by the rough air, lifting it up when it was pushed down, moving the controls with small pressures this way and that to keep the SkyFreighter on course.

A younger pilot would have wondered, Why this weather, when the forecast was clear from Portland south? But Stormy had learned early on . . . a pilot does not fly the forecast, she flies the weather that's in the sky, makes no difference it's not supposed to be there, makes no difference there's no warning of a change.

For a split moment she considered diverting from her plan, landing to repair the autopilot. In a flash of horror at the idea, though, she pushed the suggestion from her mind. She was flying to deliver her cargo to Salinas, and it would arrive at Salinas, on time, before dawn. I'll land if all four engines are on fire, she thought, or if they all quit. Otherwise, there's a mission to fly.

Outside her window, Baxter looked to heaven. His job was not going to be easy.

As she flew, Stormy Ferret considered what may have failed in the autopilot system. A tension bar broken by the shock of that hard bump, perhaps. That would make the electronics veer the plane in the opposite direction, when the failproofs would shut it down. It was a loss she could not correct from the cockpit.

Slowly fell the needle of her outside air temperature gage. When the pilot touched the ice-light switch once more, snowflakes rocketed past the wings as ever, but raindrops struck the metal and froze at once. The SkyFreighter's airspeed had dropped already, for the weight of the ice and the effect it had, dragging on the wings. Nothing about ice in the air is a friend to aviators.

She did not notice that the sudden flare of the ice-light had blinded poor Baxter, sending his helicopter spinning away, out of control.

"*Stormy!*" he cried. "*Think* before you hit the ice-light, please! Think *time for the ice-light,* please? A little warning?"

In a few seconds he could see again, and forgiving her because she did not know he was there, the angel ferret fairy closed once more on the mortal's transport.

High in the night alongside the Air Ferrets transport, Baxter thought of Willow, grieving the death of her grampa. What gift could he send, to let her know he loved her, that he wasn't dead? How could he help her understand that life does not end?

There was not enough ice, Stormy decided, that she needed to inflate the de-icing boots. She was cautious about them. On one flight she had let the ice build, and when she activated the boots, only half the system inflated. Ice on one wing and not the other. She had made it to Modesto, cargo arrived on time, but the strain of flying an unbalanced freighter had made that a flight she did not want to repeat.

"Seattle Center," she called, "Ferret Three-Five requesting seven thousand, if that's convenient."

Two thousand paws lower would increase outside air temperature by four degrees. For the time being, it would solve the icing problem, put it off till later.

"Roger, Ferret Three-Five, you can expect lower in two minutes."

"We'll expect it in two."

Once she had wondered why pilots say *we* on the radio, even when they fly alone. Me and the airplane, she had answered herself, me and my airplane is *we*.

"Stormy Ferret! It's me, Baxter, I'll be your angel ferret fairy tonight. You'll need to follow my suggestions . . ."

How pleasant it would be, she thought, if the copilot seat were not empty. Another pilot aboard to ease the burden, every half hour or so, share the task of flying by paw. And melt the loneliness. Is there no special ferret I'm destined to meet? Would that be asking too much?

"Interesting that you would mention that," said Baxter to her in his mind. "As a matter of fact, if you divert to Redding, you'll meet a flier by the name of Strobe . . ."

But there is no copilot, she told herself sternly, special ferret or otherwise, and whatever must be done to get this cargo to Salinas, I shall do by myself.

Knot my tail! thought Baxter. Why can't she *listen?* A little practice, they had told him, it's easy to talk to mortals who pay attention. What about when you haven't practiced and she doesn't care?

"Ferret Three-Five," called the Center, "you're cleared to seven thousand paws, pilot's discretion."

"Ferret Three-Five, out of nine for seven thousand."

Stormy reset the failed autopilot altitude display to *7*, pressed the control yoke forward and trimmed it to stay.

The freighter sank through the night, a thousand paws per minute, swallowed in darkness.

Frightening at first, isolated in a machine that flies, becomes deep easy pleasure with practice. Why do I love it so, she wondered, why is this fascinating? I take off into the weather, sit alone in the sky for hours, no moon, no stars sometimes, I glide down, break out of the clouds, there's the runway ahead, I land. Why does this mean so much to me?

The only others to share her peculiar loves and skills were the ferrets who fly, distinguished more by their silence in the face of visions aloft than their descriptions of what it means, to have wings. Pilots, she had noticed, rarely show their love for the calling in words.

For Stormy, flying was a mystical waterfall, a rippling enchanted mirror through which she passed every day to a different land beyond. One moment a ground creature, surveying her aircraft from a distance, the next she bound her spirit to the spirit of her airplane, the two a different being than either had been before.

"Attention, Stormy Ferret, attention, Stormy Ferret!" called Baxter. *"The next suggestion you will hear will be authorized by your guardian angel: You must land at Redding airport. You must change your destination to Redding airport! Over."*

She could not believe that other ferrets had different loves, and convinced that could only happen because the poor dears hadn't been properly introduced to the air, she resolved to make the introductions herself.

Dawns and sunsets of most every day off, she lifted young ferrets into the cabin of her own polished seaplane. She showed them how she started the engine, how to taxi from shore into the silver-blue lake by her modest home; she let them push the throttle forward, pull the control wheel back and slant them away into the sky.

"If you hear me, touch your nose," called Baxter.

The pilot flew on, paws on the control wheel.

It was as though, unable to hold the beauty of flight within her, Stormy Ferret had to give it away to love it best; unable to see flying's joy mirrored in her own eyes, it pleasured her to watch it in the eyes of others.

Such were her thoughts, as she flew. Part of her mind disciplined, intent on the business of professional flying, another part the dreamer, reliving the sparkle and flash that yesterday's seaplane flight had ignited in little Estrella Luisa Ferret, her first time in the air.

"Time for the ice-light," she thought.

Outside her window, the tiny helicopter leaped aside an instant before the beam lashed out.

"Thank you," said Baxter. *"Please confirm that you can hear me. I'm your angel ferret fairy, and I'm here with you in the night. You may not believe this, but I'm here to help . . ."*

Pilot and aircraft approached the Medford, Oregon, radio beacon, Stormy Ferret holding her SkyFreighter on course, at altitude. Beneath the clouds the foothills of the Siskiyou Mountains reached to the sky, driving moist air aloft where it would freeze at once on any moving surface. At this point, she knew, she would have to climb again, to the minimum airway altitude over the high country.

Desolate land below, she thought, and glanced at the aircraft clock. It was two-fifteen in the morning. "You can do anything with an airplane in perfect safety," her instructor had told her long ago, "until you hit the ground."

Stormy had never hit the ground except for gently, wheels first, on a runway. She was not interested in trying any other way.

A different channel, thought Baxter. She won't take my help, but perhaps she'll help me. *"What gift can I bring to my Willow?"* he called. *"She thinks I've left her. She thinks I'm dead!"*

A moment of old memory, then all at once came to Stormy's mind the helmet and goggles her father had given her when she was a sky-struck kit. He wouldn't take his first airplane ride until he flew with his daughter when she got her Ferret Cub, but one day, no reason except that he loved her, he had brought home a flying helmet and goggles for her, bought for pennies at a used-thing store.

How she had treasured them! Her father's love had transfigured the gift. Helmet and goggles, she had worn them on her first solo flight, kept them still, cherished them now more than ever.

Seattle Center called, breaking the dream. "Ferret Three-Five, you're cleared to one-one thousand, eleven thousand paws crossing the Rogue Valley VOR."

"Ferret Three-Five," she replied, "out of seven thousand for one-one thousand, eleven thousand."

The awkward official wording came when a pilot cleared to climb to one-one thousand paws misunderstood, began descending instead to one thousand, saw mountaintop where he expected sky. Every rule of the air, they say, was born in somebody's mistake.

Now the hard part begins, she thought, now I shall earn my keep. She advanced all throttles for her climb. At that instant the number four engine misfired, its smooth drone broken into irregular trembling. Stormy felt it through the control yoke in her paw, pushed the engine's fuel-mixture lever forward till it smoothed.

"That's not right," she said.

"Hello, Nimble," Baxter called ahead on the fairy communication frequency. "Are we failing her number four engine? I thought we were doing the weather, just the weather. It's a little dangerous, isn't it, to fail her engine up here?"

On the airway south, Nimble and Prestor had done a fine job with the storm. The energy of the Shasta Vortex exploded warm air aloft as from an invisible volcano. When they uncapped the energy of the Tahoe Vortex and turned it north, it was fuel to a fire—lightning-forks everywhere, searing branches ripped and split through a towering electric forest.

"Of course we're not failing her engine, Baxter," Nimble called over the thunders. "And don't you do it. She's going to need all the power she can get!"

Esther, the energy boss, gave a cool warning from her helicopter high over the Sierra as the Yosemite Vortex broke loose. "Attention all angel ferret personnel, we have a force ten burst heading three-five-five, locked on the force eight aloft. All units remain clear until impact." Then, seeing the cloud-fires boiling from the horizon: *"Here she comes, gentlefairies! Half Dome's coming at you!"*

Nimble saw it streaking toward him from the south, an avalanche of tortured air from sea level to nearly eighty thousand paws, twisting rolls of cumulus rimmed in blue fire, tumbling up the airway at the speed of heat. When that force met the storm they had already cooked, over the Siskiyou . . .

He rolled and dived to the north, eyes like dinner plates. "Let's get out of here, Prestor!"

His partner agreed, the two golden machines darting full throttle up the airway toward Stormy's airplane, surfing the shock wave of the monster they had created.

"Baxter!" called Nimble as they flew. "We may have overdone the storm. It's got a long way to go but it's coming awfully fast . . ."

Stormy glanced at the number four fuel-pressure gage. Wavering, just a little. At the number four oil pressure. Was it trembling as well, ever so slightly? She looked to her right, across the flight deck and out the window toward engine number four. No sparks, no fires, nothing out there but darkness.

Airplane crashes never happen by themselves, she knew, they always end a chain of events, and every takeoff of every flight is the beginning of a chain. These were the links that she had accepted:

She had taken off,
she was flying alone,
on instruments,
at night,
with a failed autopilot,
climbing into known icing,
over rugged terrain,
toward uncertain weather.

The next link, she thought:
with an engine that could fail at any time.

It didn't take imagination to finish the accident report: *The pilot was unable to feather the propeller of her failed engine. The aircraft, with a heavy load of ice, lost altitude until it contacted mountainous terrain.*

She double-checked the propeller anti-ice switches: *On,* hoped the electrics were warming the heavy blades against the cold ahead.

Everyone knows it's a pilot's job to break chains before crashes can happen, she thought. Yet a professional knows as well that it's her job to fly her cargo south, to get it there by dawn.

Stormy frowned, pulled the control yoke back, the slightest of pressures, and the SkyFreighter began to climb. This leg is the worst. It'll be a while before we're out of the mountains.

It took a minute longer to climb than she had planned, and by the time she leveled, ice was building steadily on the wings. The airspeed was down considerably. When she snapped on the light, she knew what she would see: ice a blanket over the curve of the metal surface, dazzling as angels' wings, a brilliant glare in the night.

The number four engine choked, recovered.

Stormy was a busy ferret in the cockpit, too busy to be frightened. She increased the carburetor heat to all engines and ran it full hot to number four. The engine gasped again and smoothed.

"Stormy," called Baxter. "Try to hear me. In two minutes . . . well, we're sorry but in two minutes it's going to be a little rough up here. All of us hope you could divert to Redding airport . . ."

Time to blow the boots, she thought, and pressed the switch to inflate the wing de-ice system. At once, ice like sheets of plate glass exploded from the transport's wings, shattering behind her into the night, dark silver knives spinning away.

If he hadn't already crossed the Rainbow Bridge, the eruption of razor edges through his helicopter would have taken Baxter there in the twitch of a tail. As it was, he dodged by reflex, never quite knowing whether he had missed the explosion or if the glowing daggers had passed harmlessly through the helicopter and his own body.

Everything's okay, he thought, everything's going according to plan. One minute to go.

"Come on, Stormy," the cargo pilot said aloud, "let's settle down. Everything's okay, it's just another flight. This is just one more flight."

Had she been watching with a different sense, she would have seen the rendezvous: her transport lumbering ahead, two angel ferret fairies fleeing backward from their own storm, a runaway freight train the size of Sicily.

Nimble and Prestor turned to join the transport, flew ahead of it by a hundred paws. They would meet the chaos an instant before the SkyFreighter.

Baxter closed on the cockpit, peered through the glass at Stormy Ferret.

She's going to share my Willow's destiny, he thought.

While she watched her flight instruments, he watched her dark eyes, felt her thoughts, the connection between them slowly opening.

"Tell her to hang on," Nimble panted. "We had to do it. What's coming at us, if I say so myself, pretty soon she'll change her mind . . ."

"It's her destiny," said Prestor, his best apology. "She's got to meet Strobe!"

Gently as he could, Baxter flew yet closer to the cockpit, reached for Stormy's mind with his own: Everything's going to be all right. But you must land, you must land at Redding!

Nimble's voice: "Here we go!"

"Stormy!" shouted Baxter to the mortal in the cockpit. *"You've got to land!"*

It was like nothing she had ever struck in the air. Stormy flew her SkyFreighter head-on into air torn to tumbling blocks by the updrafts, into Niagaras by the downdrafts, copper lightning forking swords and spears around her, her wings struck once and again, holes melted through metal.

Almost never does a pilot hear thunder in the cockpit; it crashed in now, time and again. So ferociously was her transport shaken by the tempest that the instrument panel shivered to an unrelenting blur.

Had she looked out her window that moment with serene and loving spirit, Stormy would have seen a tiny helicopter yanked upward by the violent air, would have seen it reappear for an instant by her window as the pilot fought for control, then disappear, yanked downward out of sight.

Not expecting angel ferret fairies beside her window, however, she did not turn to look. She gripped the control wheel tightly in her paws, hauling what she could see of the artificial horizon back to what she hoped might be level flight.

The windshield ahead had long since frozen over; she did nothing to clear it, halfway expecting the shaking to crack the ice, the other half expecting the windshield itself to disappear.

She pressed the microphone button on her control yoke, fought to hold it down. Her message sounded like a voice from a paint-shaker: "Seattle Center, Ferret Three-Five. We're picking up a little ice and a bit of a rough ride. Be advised we'd like a lower altitude, soon as that might be convenient for you."

Baxter appeared again by her window, gesturing, pointing. *"Down!"* Then he was hurled away.

Far below, a controller ferret watched his radar screen, responded to her call. "Ferret Three-Five, this is Seattle Center. The best we can give you is one-zero thousand, ten thousand paws, if that would help."

"It would."

"Tell him to warn her!" called Baxter. "Nimble, tell the controller to warn her!"

"Ferret Three-Five," said Seattle Center, "you are cleared pilot's discretion to one-zero thousand, ten thousand paws."

Ten thousand paws was still above the freezing level, the ice building as fast as ever in the storm. With every cycle of the boots, it was as though the SkyFreighter had flown through some vast show window aloft, great shards and fragments shearing away, glittering, falling.

Ten thousand paws was a joke. Stormy could no more hold an altitude in the hurricane than she could read the jackhammer instrument panel.

"Sorry our radar isn't much good for weather, Air Ferret," said the Center, "but it looks something fierce from your position all the way down Victor Two-Three."

She didn't reply. Captain Janine Ferret fought to hold her aircraft on course, ice erupting now and then from her wings, Baxter striving to stay up with her transport, to change the pilot's mind, Nimble and Prestor in their own little helicopters beyond the SkyFreighter's wingtips, hanging on.

Bell-balls a crazed melody, as though the cargo plane had become some mad sleigh bounding out of control on snow boulders ten thousand paws high.

On the transport's unprotected surfaces—the nose cone, the propeller domes, the radio antennas, the tips of the elevators and rudders—ice built unceasingly.

Gradually the tempest gained the upper paw. Stormy gave up her fight to maintain altitude, set herself simply to hold her freighter right-side up, letting the gale hammer-toss her where it would.

She clenched her teeth, one moment her body squashed flat, the next, jammed hard against her safety belt, the pilot ignoring part within her that knew she'd had enough, tonight. Had-enough makes no difference, she thought. One can't give up. One must fly the aircraft.

Shaken in the skyquake, she thought of her seaplane, safe in the hangar at home; in a few days' time she'd be flying kits again on their first rides. In spite of the battering, as she burst the ice away from her wings yet again, she smiled at that.

Stormy thought for a long moment before calling the Center. It was her habit to understate reports of turbulence and ice, but she couldn't allow another pilot to fly this route unwarned. Any lesser machine than a Ferret SkyFreighter would be torn asunder.

Deciding to call, her paw was jerked from the microphone button. No! Gripping the wheel firmly in both paws, she braced for the updraft that was sure to follow. It did, snapping her head down as it blew the transport straight up.

"Seattle . . ."

For three seconds the sky went flare-white around her, not a bolt of lightning but a sheet of it, blinding. She flew the airplane by feel, waiting for sight to return.

Over the roar of engines and storm, the ferret captain heard a crash in the cargo bay behind her, a freight pallet breaking loose inside the containers. Not good. If a container itself failed in this weather, it would be thrown through the fuselage, and that would be the end.

Mountains slid below, heavy and slow as solid rock. With great difficulty, her paw continually jerked from the selector panel, Stormy changed to the Oakland Center radio frequency, desperate for a warmer, smoother lower altitude.

The radio antennas did not have de-icing boots. She was reminded of this by a call from Center.

"Ferret Three-Five, this is Oakland Center. Be advised there's a new SigMet Alpha One for convec—"

She finished the warning in her mind, guessing that the sudden silence was not a Center radio failure but an iced antenna torn away from her airplane. The radio was dead, not a sound save for a roll of static, white noise matching the wild blizzard outside.

She didn't need a warning to tell her of the SIGnificant METeorological conditions, as air-talk so delicately put it, for she had no hope of escape. The shortest way out of difficult weather is straight ahead.

The SkyFreighter plowed the whirling air like a tramp steamer through a typhoon at sea, pitching, thudding, rolling in the dark. The pilot switched to the number two radio, unsure how long its antenna would survive the ice.

"Hi, Center, Ferret Three-Five."

"Ferret Three-Five, acknowledge the SigMet."

"We're in the SigMet!" she said, suddenly cross. "We've lost our primary radio antenna; be advised that if we lose the number two, we will proceed as filed to Salinas."

It was standard procedure, but she wanted it on the record. She carried a battery-powered backup radio in her flight bag and thought tonight may be the night that she would need it.

"Roger Three-Five. Salinas weather is wind calm, measured five hundred paws, overcast, light rain, fog . . ."

She nodded. Of course, she thought. Center was hinting that Salinas weather was worse than forecast, that she might divert to an easier landing place.

"Yes!" cried Baxter. *"Divert! This will not look good on the accident report, that you continued . . ."*

Even my mind is playing tricks tonight. She clung to the control wheel. Everybody wants me to quit. A grim smile. Not likely.

She chose not to quit, aware that she was adding one more link to her chain: *Pilot declined opportunity of precautionary landing after storm damaged her aircraft.*

The cargo plane skidded and shuddered through a sky blacker and rougher than any Stormy had known, her charts and clipboard thrown across the flight deck, strewn back again. Her course was memorized, but as far as she knew, there was no one else over the Siskiyou tonight, no one so crazy to be here.

Not so, she thought, tightening her shoulder harness as hard as it could go. She gripped the wheel for the next careening blow. Not crazy. Determined.

"Nimble! Prestor!" called Baxter, his voice jagged in the storm. "She's set her mind, she's going to take it through! *Rougher! More turbulence!*"

Prestor called back, "We're full-out, Baxter! *We can't make it any worse!*"

Minutes were months. The SkyFreighter flew as if it were a truck run away on great square wheels, off the road, down a mountainside. Stormy's jaw ached from clenching shut, she barely remembered what an altimeter looked like that wasn't blurred just this side of invisible.

In the midst, her artificial-horizon indicator tumbled, the gyro thrown beyond its limits, screaming that the

SkyFreighter was upside down and spinning. "No, you don't," said the pilot. She pulled its reset knob; the swirling instrument recovered.

In the cargo compartment, a second pallet failed, and a third. But the pilot was locked on her mission. If she lost the rudder itself, she would still fly her transport straight ahead, she'd steer with the engines, if she had to.

The calm voice of the controller, down in his calm radar room: "Ferret Three-Five, you are cleared to nine thousand paws reaching Shasta Intersection. Say the nature of your weather, please."

"Oakland Center, Ferret Three-Five," she replied, out of breath. "We've got heavy mixed rime and clear icing. And severe to extreme turbulence . . ."

Shasta Intersection was still long minutes to the south, hard granite patiently below, waiting.

In the midst of her struggle, the ferret watched the number four engine gages, blinked quickly to freeze an image of the shuddering dials. Oil pressure was down, all right. Above minimum pressure, it was, but down a needle-width on the instrument. A needle-width low on the oil pressure, that's a whisper to a pilot that something unpleasant is about to happen. A whisper lost. Stormy refused to believe that an engine would fail when so much else was tearing loose.

Almost to Shasta Intersection, Stormy thought, though it wasn't true.

She groped for the de-ice switch once more, pressed it, and instead of sheets of ice flying away, the de-ice circuit breaker failed.

Fang, she thought, hanging on to the control wheel against the avalanche outside. This is not what we need.

It took a long time to reset the circuit breaker, her paw missing it again and again for the SkyFreighter's bucking and rolling. Then she pressed the de-ice switch, nodded briefly at the welcome shower of ice from the wings. After a few seconds, though, the breaker failed again. Add that to your chain, she thought: *de-icing equipment failed.*

"Almost to Shasta," she said aloud.

Ice building, her airplane slowed. The number four engine is ready to fail, she thought, the autopilot's gone, main radio antenna's gone, standby radio is ready to fail, ice-protection system is telling me good-bye. Not many links left, before the crash.

With a minute to go, she pulled the number four throttle back by a quarter.

"Oakland Center," she called. "Ferret Three-Five is Shasta Intersection, out of ten thousand for nine."

There was no answer from Center. Nor did she hear any word from them, second after second.

"Oakland, this is Ferret Three-Five, radio check."

Not a sound.

The number two antenna had failed. She shrugged. No matter. I am out of this to nine thousand.

It was easy to lose the altitude, the frozen transport not much willing to fly.

I should have climbed, she thought. First thing, I saw ice, I should have climbed as high as I could go. Get that outside air temperature colder than twenty below, I could have flown above the ice. She blinked. Wouldn't have worked. Updrafts carry the cold water higher, the icing would have been worse, would have forced me down.

Considering this, down she came, Stormy Ferret in the thundering silence of her transport.

Outside her window, Baxter watched it all slip away. The pilot had made it through the worst the AFF Task Force could throw, she was almost in the clear.

"Stormy!" shouted the angel ferret fairy. Then, desperate: *"Janine! For Willow's sake! Land now!"*

She heard the sound of it in her mind, a clear, strange voice. Then she tossed her head, shook the words away.

All at once, as she descended, pandemonium ceased, her square-wheel truck vaulted off its boulder-field mountainside to skate on tilted glass. Ghost-blue light fluttered on the frozen windshield. Gentle, soft. Static-electric fingers pressing the skin of the freighter.

Her snowy face turned cobalt in the light, reflecting the eerie glow through half a paw of ice on the windshield. Any other animal would have burst into tears, grateful for the calm. Stormy sighed happily. What a wonder, she thought, an instrument panel I can see!

Most of the instrument lights had failed, broken glass on the floor of the flight deck. She flew by the dome light, overhead.

The outside air temperature was up to two degrees centigrade. She would not have to climb into the ice again, all the way to Salinas. Reckless, she pressed the wing de-ice switch. Nothing happened but the silent pop of the circuit breaker. The system was lost.

She reached to the floor behind her, where her flight bag had been thrown by the violence. From a zippered pocket, just under the crystal-covered propeller of her first model airplane, she took her pawheld radio, attached its antenna, pressed its tiny speaker under her headphones.

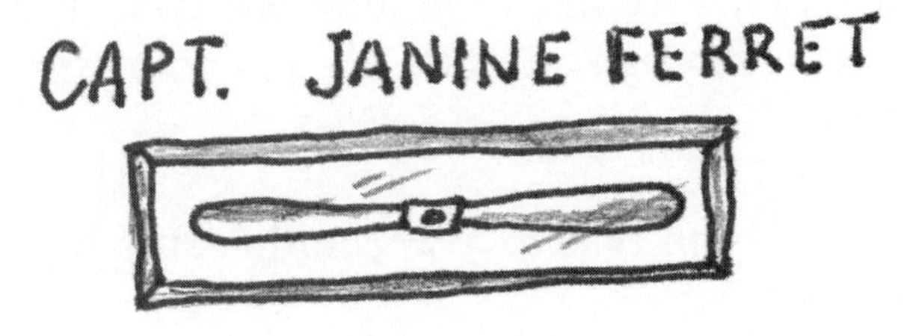

"Hello, Oakland Center, how do you hear Ferret Three-Five?"

"Ferret Three-Five, Oakland Center, we read you four-by-four. Go ahead."

The animal relaxed, letting go tensions she had not known she was holding. "Oakland, Ferret Three-Five is level at nine thousand paws, requesting eight."

As if there had been no problem, as indeed there had not been in the quiet radar rooms of Oakland Center, the voice, affable, was happy to help. "Ferret Three-Five, cleared pilot's discretion to eight thousand paws, Red Bluff altimeter two-nine-five-two."

The captain acknowledged this, eased her transport down into the warmer air. At eight thousand paws, the first sheet of ice ripped away from the wings, its grip melting away. Then, windshield ice broke and disappeared, first a tiny patch, then instantly the whole surface was clear, rain once more spraying the glass.

In the beam of her ice-light, the snow was gone, just raindrops streaking through the dark. She did not notice small helicopters.

"We've failed," said Baxter. "We couldn't stop her. She's going through!"

"Can't win 'em all," said Prestor. "I've seen it before. Sometimes they get so stubborn there's nothing we can do, nothing their guardian angels can do. They're not asking guidance, not their highest right, even. Stormy's decided her destiny is to get her cargo through. Not to meet Strobe, not to change the world."

"We only suggest," said Nimble. "She's the mortal. She decides."

"But my Willow . . ."

"Your grandkit will be all right," said Prestor softly, as though he knew something that Baxter didn't.

Stormy held the number four engine at low cruise. If it could keep running, she'd prefer to have it with her, in case she missed the instrument approach at Salinas.

A new voice on the radio:

"Oakland Center, MusTel Two-Zero. We're abeam Redding, out of seven thousand paws for one-two thousand, twelve thousand, Medford next. And you might advise your southbound aircraft of severe weather through Sacramento."

Stormy blinked, unbelieving. Medford next? This pilot is going to fly through the same sky that shredded my SkyFreighter?

The angel ferret fairies heard the call.

"It's him!" said Baxter. "It's Strobe!"

Stormy waited for the Center to advise MusTel 20 that an Air Ferrets SkyFreighter had reported severe to extreme turbulence, heavy icing, on the route ahead.

They did not. She waited. Had the shift changed at Center, the new controller unaware of her report?

She pressed her microphone button. "Oakland Center, Air Ferret Three-Five with a message for MusTel Two-Zero, if he can read my transmitter."

"MusTel Two-Zero, do you read Air Ferret Three-Five?" said the Center controller. "She's got a message for you."

The voice came back, broken as though the pilot's paw had been pulled from the microphone button. "I read you four square, Air— Air Ferret. Go ahead."

Stormy made it short: "MusTel, Air Ferret's a SkyFreighter southbound on Victor Two-Three. If you intend airway Victor Two-Three to Medford, be advised there's extreme weather on that route. I got heavy ice at one-one thousand, turbulence broke the cargo loose, unable to maintain altitude in the shear."

"Roger, Air Ferret. If you're southbound on Victor Two-Three, you've got a prob—"

Then silence. Had MusTel lost an antenna, too?

Then the same voice, on a different transmitter. Something had happened to his primary radio. "Oakland Center, MusTel Two-Zero's requesting vectors to the back course at Redding. We'll divert to Redding."

"Roger, MusTel. Confirm you're canceling your destination Medford."

"That is affirmative. We are canceling destination Medford, diverting to Redding. We'll let the storm have Victor Two-Three for a while."

"Roger. MusTel Two-Zero, turn right heading one-seven-five, expect the Redding Localizer/DME Back Course Runway One-Six approach, maintain seven thousand paws, expect lower shortly."

The MusTel pilot read back the clearance, a voice remarkably calm, Stormy thought, for somebody turning about in the storm that had just torn pieces off her airplane.

Then he called again. "Center, this is MusTel Two-Zero. You might advise Air Ferret she's got a bit of bad weather down Victor Two-Three southbound. We left a little paint on the hail, back there. I know it's Sacramento, but there's hooks all over my radar, it's a pretty wild ride."

Together the three angel ferret fairies screamed to the pilot, *"Divert, Stormy Ferret! DIVERT NOW!"*

She sighed, listened to the faintest voice of her highest right. To fight through one runaway cold front was noble under the circumstances, she thought. To survive one and immediately take on another, that would not look good on the accident report.

All at once, she was exhausted.

"Hi, Oakland," she called. Words she had never spoken before: "Air Ferret Three-Five, we'll divert. We're canceling our destination Salinas, requesting direct Redding for the Back Course One-Six and a full stop Redding."

"Roger, Three-Five, we have your cancellation Salinas. You're cleared present position direct the Redding VOR, expect the Redding Localizer/DME Back Course Runway One-Six approach, maintain eight thousand paws, lower shortly."

"Three-Five," said Stormy, "present position direct the VOR and the loke-demi Back Course One-Six, maintaining eight."

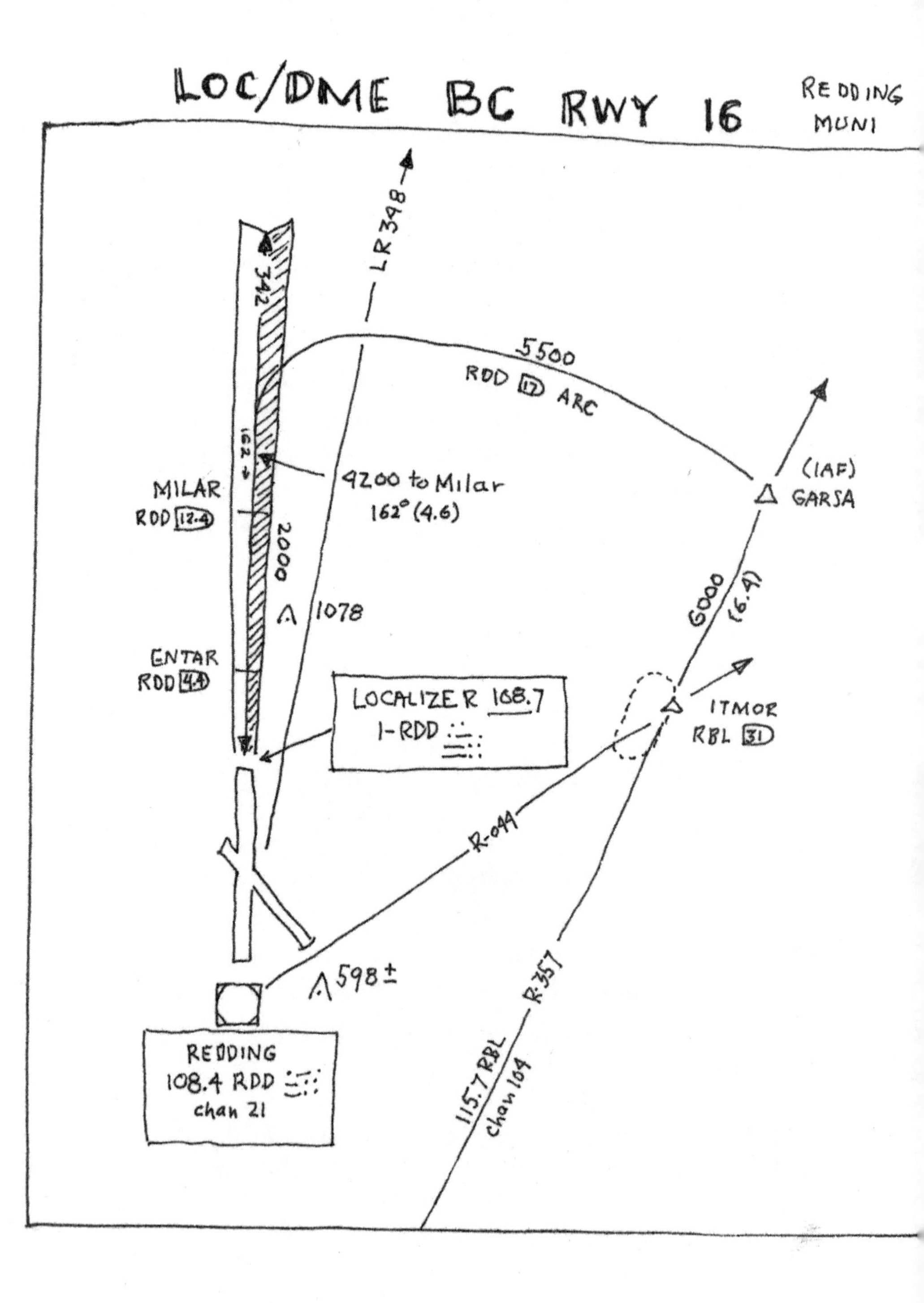

LOC/DME BC RWY 16
REDDING MUNI
LR348
342
5500
RDD 17 ARC
(IAF)
GARSA
162
MILAR
RDD 12.4
4200 to Milar
162° (4.6)
2000
1078
6000
(6.4)
ENTAR
RDD 4.4
LOCALIZER 108.7
I-RDD
ITMOR
RBL 31
R-044
598±
REDDING
108.4 RDD
chan 21
R-357
115.7 RBL
chan 104

The fairies were wild with joy, looping and rolling their helicopters around the SkyFreighter, sparkling trails of fairy dust behind, barely missing the spinning propellers.

"Mission accomplished," said Nimble. *"Mission accomplished!"*

Likewise had Gnat's despair been turned to triumph. Flying close formation with Strobe, Goosebeak had failed, had been unable to force the pilot to divert any more than Baxter could convince Stormy. The fairy breathed a prayer of thanks and rightness. The only force that could change these minds was the power of the other mortal's suggestion.

Stormy turned her SkyFreighter toward the Redding Omnirange, found the approach plate, LOC/DME BC RWY 16, the instrument procedure for weather landings, clipped it to her control wheel, gave it a quick study, reading aloud.

"Fly outbound on the zero-four-four degree radial to the Itmor intersection, thence maintain six thousand paws out the three-five-seven degree radial of Red Bluff to the Garsa intersection, thence a descending arc on the Redding beacon to intercept the localizer, thence cross Milar at forty-two hundred paws, cross Entar at two thousand, descend to the missed approach point at nine-two-zero paws to land."

She nodded, remembering. She had flown it before—not the easiest approach in the world, not the most difficult.

Miles ahead of her, the whisper of jet engines behind his flight deck, Strobe Ferret studied the same diagram. At the touch of a button his global positioning system showed the path to follow, outlined headings and altitudes in glowing color on the panel before him. He touched a lighted square on his panel and the autopilot turned the FerrJet to fly the approach on its own.

Soon he was slanting down past Garsa intersection, the Center handing him off: "MusTel Two-Zero, contact Redding Tower intercepting the localizer. Have a good morning."

Strobe wondered, every time a controller spoke them, why the four extra words? Everyone's in charge of their own morning, why would we have a bad one? But those seconds spent on the same words, over and over, they add up. It's a long wait to sunrise, he concluded. The controller's lonely.

The FerrJet sighing down through the arc of the approach, Strobe relaxed in his scarf of midnight and gold stripes, monitoring the autopilot as it intercepted the final approach course. He thought of the weekend ahead, four kits eager to ride in the biplane. Of course they'll need to wash it first, and they'll need to learn the names of all its parts.

In a sudden blink of a world returning, MusTel 20 broke out of the bottom of the clouds, twin rows of runway lights directly ahead.

With the touch of a paw on the control wheel, Strobe disconnected the autopilot, tilted the jet's nose upward ever so slightly as it descended, let the main wheels chirp on the rain-slick runway, gentled the nosewheel down a few seconds later, pulled the thrust levers into reverse.

"MusTel Two-Zero, turn right at the next intersection," said the ferret controller in the tower. "Say your destination on the airport."

"Transient parking. I'll just be an hour."

"Roger, Two-Zero. Taxi to transient parking, remain this frequency."

"Two-Zero, roger," said Strobe. "May's Diner open?"

"Twenty-four hours, Captain."

Stopped on the parking ramp, MusTelCo's chief pilot pulled the FerrJet's thrust levers back to *Off,* listening to the music of its engines whispering into silence.

He finished shutting down his airplane to the drum of rain on the windshield and fuselage, filled out squares in the aircraft log. Then, removing his headset and midnight-gold scarf, he rose and set a cap of tattered red corduroy upon his head, pulled the earflaps down against the rain outside.

Pressing the *Door-open* switch by the exit, the pilot padded down the stairs, turned as soon as his paws touched the ground and moved the *Door-close* lever up.

He did not notice the golden helicopter hovering at his shoulder as he walked to May's Diner. Nor did he hear Gnat's soft call on the AFF frequency as he entered the restaurant: *"Goosebeak is in the Birdcage, Goosebeak is in the Birdcage . . ."*

At that moment, the nose of the Air Ferrets SkyFreighter broke through the bottom of the clouds, the same patient runway lights stretching ahead.

Stormy double-checked three green lights, landing gear down and locked. What a flight, she thought. Good decision. Bella will be working at the hangar, this hour, she can replace the antenna and take a look at the number four engine. Secure the cargo, a snack at May's, and off to Salinas. I'll be late, but still before dawn.

A second later the tires of the SkyFreighter whispered against the glistening runway, a puff of steam, then spray flying as they touched.

Stormy eased the nosewheel down, moved the flap lever up, and as her airplane slowed, tapped the brakes. Slowing with her, the three angel ferret fairies air-taxied alongside.

"Air Ferret Three-Five, turn right at the next intersection," came the voice from the tower. "You can taxi to transient parking, remain this frequency." A pause, then: "Is that you, Stormy?"

The pilot smiled, considered that at this hour she did not have to stick so close to rules. She pressed the microphone button. “Hi, Bart. I’ll taxi to the Air Ferrets hangar, if I can. A little wild weather for you tonight?”

“You’re cleared to the Air Ferrets hangar, Stormy,” he said. “A little wild? Oh, yes! Without our shields we’d have lost the glass!”

CHAPTER 4

THE THREE angel ferret fairies hovered near the Sky-Freighter's wingtip, resting in the air while Stormy found Bella, mentioned her problems with the transport.

How difficult that was, Baxter thought. The truth is that there's nothing we did to stop her from flying south, past the one who will be the love of her life. Why do mortals so resist their own beautiful destinies? Why couldn't I have whispered, instead of screaming at her? Why couldn't she *listen?*

He wasn't expecting an answer, so new an angel ferret fairy that he had forgotten that life was different on this level. Here, every question asked is answered.

"We can only suggest to our mortals," he heard the voice of his own mind, drawing from a deeper well of knowing. "Sometimes they're distracted by the seems-to-be. Sometimes they forget what good can happen when they listen within."

I used to be distracted, too, Baxter thought. So easy it is to mistake task for purpose.

"All of you working together," the voice went on, "all your powers together, you couldn't force them to choose. But you caught her attention tonight, and Gnat caught Strobe's. They decided on their own."

Baxter's helicopter trembled in the air. How do I know this? Is it you? My own guardian angel still with me, though I'm an angel now, myself?

"With you, and always will be." Baxter listened, filled with delight at what he heard. "The most powerful souls accept the most humble places. You're an angel ferret fairy, you and your flying friends. You're more, as well, you're infinitely more. Keep following your own right, Bax, no matter what, and watch how lovely it is, your life unfolding before you!"

"You'll never leave?"

"You can tune me out. You're always free not to listen. But never can the bond to our highest self be broken."

For the first time, Baxter understood what he had not asked. Even you! he thought, even you have your own guardian angel!

He sensed that the voice was smiling. "Even me."

And your guardian angel?

"She has her guides, too. We all do. We're all guides, one to another, on a thousand different levels. As we are led, so do we lead our own dear others."

But . . .

"Bax. Listen." There was a long moment of quiet, the fairy eager to hear. *"As I am to you, so are you to little Willow."*

Baxter caught his breath and understood. *I'm Willow's guardian angel!* He imagined his own guardian-angel ferret, a creature of glory, eyes of love, fur of pure spun light, sitting alongside him in the helicopter.

You're . . . beautiful!

"So are you, dear Baxter! Have your forgotten? We don't become beautiful as we grow. We realize that we've been beautiful all along."

He blinked, and when he looked again, the angel was gone.

"I'm not gone," said the voice within.

CHAPTER 5

MASKLESS, eyes the color of coals, fur white as fine linen, Bella Ferret lifted a new radio antenna in her paw, moved a wheeled scaffold to the SkyFreighter.

"Say, Captain," she called to the pilot in the cargo bay, where Stormy worked to secure a container that had been ripped from its tie-downs, "what does an albino ferret say when you blow in her ear?"

Stormy stopped and leaned out the cargo door, smiling down at her friend. "I don't know, Bella. What does an albino ferret say when you blow in her ear?"

"Thanks for the refill!"

Stormy laughed. "Oh, Bella! Will you ever run out of dumb-albino jokes?"

"I'd doubt that, Cap. I didn't used to could spell *albino,* and now I *are* one!"

Cargo secured, Bella working to replace the antenna, Stormy climbed down the ladder and set off in cap and scarf through the rain toward May's, trailing three tiny helicopters in her wake.

Between the hangar and the diner was parked a sleek FerrJet, royal blues and whites sparkling in the ramp lights, golden *MusTelCo* on the vertical stabilizer. The paint on the leading edge of the wings and tail Stilton Ferret had been peeled as though sandblasted. A mechanic was inside, nose and whiskers disappeared in the space behind the aft cabin.

That will cost a bit, repainting, she thought, and smiled. What a life Stilton Ferret must lead!

Yet she was just as happy tonight not to be the world's richest ferret. So much happier she was, battling weather and schedules in her airplane than ever she would be, some helpless magnate blown by winds of business and privilege.

She wondered where the pilot had gone, the one who had taken her advice not to continue. Whose advice not to continue she had taken, as well.

"Not here," whispered Baxter, eager to whisk her along. Then he relaxed. I can only suggest.

Off in the limousine to his suite, she guessed.

Not admitting fatigue even to herself, for her flight was not finished, Stormy climbed the three steps to May's, her fur beaded with rain, sparkling like diamonds.

The place was empty, save for May herself at the last booth, a fluffy ball of champagne fur, talking with a shabby-looking ferret in a rag hat.

The owner glanced up when the bell chimed over the door.

"Bless my burrow!" she called. "If it isn't Miss Stormy Ferret herself!"

She didn't notice three golden rotorcraft at the edge of a shared dimension, whirling through the door after Stormy, spiraling down one after another to land by Gnat's helicopter on the tabletop.

Stormy smiled to see her, hugged her old friend. "May! What are you doing here before dawn? Fine restaurants at every airport, she can't afford to sleep?"

The round ferret laughed. "I knew you'd be at Redding tonight, kit, so I rushed on down to fix your breakfast!"

"Oh, May. I didn't know I'd be here myself till Mr. Stilton Ferret out there suggested I'd save some paint if I landed for a bit. Can you imagine a storm like that, a wild storm over *Sacramento?* This is the first time I've ever landed for weather. First time!"

Stormy nodded to the animal in the booth. In front of him was a cup of hot chocolate, a plate of toast and pickles. He nodded back.

It wasn't the ferret that was scruffy, she noticed, it was his hat. Ragged earflaps askew, stitched together in patches, rain-soaked. The creature himself, dark fur touched with silver, was not unattractive.

She smiled. "Nice hat," she said.

"My goodness," said May. "Stormy, don't you know this ferret? Stormy, this is Strobe; Strobe, meet Stormy. Can't believe you haven't met!" She wiped her paws on her apron. "What can I get for you, kit? The usual?"

So his name is Strobe. "Thank you, May," she said. "I'll just be a bit, then I'm off again when the weather moves through."

The proprietress bustled away, a hidden smile, determined to take her time with the order. Bless my burrow. Who would have thought these two had never met?

The other ferret rose. "Would you care to join me, Miss Stormy?"

"Janine's my real name. I don't have the sense to come in out of the rain, so they call me Stormy. Tell me about your hat."

"It would be my pleasure." Is it the raindrop diamonds, Strobe thought, or her dramatic entrance from the night . . . what is it about her? Confidence? Knowing? There's a serenity here. Then he gave up descriptions and accepted that here was the most beautiful animal he had ever seen.

He recovered, not wanting to stare. Thinking fast under pressure was second nature. He glanced at the table-side music box, jotted something on a napkin, turned it over. He dropped a coin in the machine. "You choose," he said.

"Why, thank you, sir." She didn't have to turn the index cards to find her favorite. She pressed button *F* and button *7*. "I love this song."

In the moment before the music began, Strobe turned the napkin. On it was written *F-7*.

F-6: WILD FERRET

-ZSA-ZSA AND THE SHOW FERRETS-

F-7: IF I COULD FLY

Stormy looked up, caught her breath.

The ferret dropped his jaw in a look of wonder, he couldn't believe his own amazing powers. "Why, it's Zsa-Zsa and the Show Ferrets!" he said. "'If I Could Fly.'" Then he smiled, suddenly shy, gave away the secret. "What else would you pick?"

Stormy, charmed, didn't know what to say. It was a lovely ballad, Chloe Ferret's voice a low, haunting chime, Zsa-Zsa and Misty echoing the notes behind. "'Feathers for fur,'" she hummed along, "'wings grown from my shoulders . . .'" He must love it, too.

Strobe considered telling her that his friend Boa, of the Ferret Rescue Service, knew Chloe, that he knew her quite well. Next he thought he might ask if Stormy had heard that humans choose ferret musicians to play backup on fully 80 percent of the music they record in studios. But he remained silent before this radiant new acquaintance, watching her eyes.

"Your hat's been with you for a while," she prompted.

"Oh!" He was caught off balance by her words. He removed it, examined it as though for the first time, set it on the seat beside him. "It's my second hat, actually. I had to retire the first one. It was getting a few too many hours on it."

She raised her eyebrows, interested. Only pilots talk of hours on things.

"You fly, do you?"

He nodded. "Some. I guess you do, too."

"SkyFreighters. For Air Ferrets."

"So you're the freight dog!" he said, one of the few times in his life he spoke before he thought. It's a term of respect, he chafed at himself, she knows that's how I mean it. "There's work for the adventurous. I used to have the courage for that. Long ago."

She liked his manner. "Where did you fly?"

"East Coast, mostly. Rochester–Albany–New Haven. Allentown–Pittsburgh–Chicago . . ."

". . . Cleveland–Erie–Rochester?" she asked.

"Pretty well."

Some of the worst weather in the world. "My hat's off to you, Mr. Strobe."

"Why, thank you. I could use one."

They laughed together.

Unstrapped from their machines, watching now from the tabletop, the four angel ferret fairies nudged each other happily.

May brought Stormy's order, warm ferret food and mountain-snow water. "Here you go, darlin'. You enjoy that."

The water glass came down perilously close to Baxter's helicopter, and he pushed his rotorcraft farther down-table, out of the way. The other fairies watched and smiled. Old habits die hard.

Stormy looked up at her friend. "Thanks, May."

"You're a healthy one, I'd guess," said Strobe.

"I wish I could guess the same for you. That's not much nutrition, is it, toast and pickles?"

He touched his plate toward her. "Care for a bite?"

"No thanks. Behind the bell-balls, I've got thirty cases of ferret food aboard for Salinas." She smiled at him. "I believe in my cargo."

The angel ferret fairies looked at each other. "Operation Midnight Snack, mission accomplished," said Gnat. "They're going to love each other." He yawned and stretched. "Congratulations, Nimble. Great work, Prestor. You did a good job, too, Baxter, your first time out. Very good job."

"How about pears?" asked Strobe. There had to be some way to see her again.

"Pears?"

"Ever tasted a Sultana pear?" I could talk with her forever, if only she weren't mid-rush, ready to fly away.

"No, as a matter of fact, I haven't. What's a Sultana pear?"

"Friend of mine has orchards, not far from Medford. Sultanas . . . well, I can't quite describe them. They taste . . . they're firm, sweet, juicy clouds."

She looked at him, startled, pleased at the language. How nice it would be to know this one, she thought, if he weren't waiting on the storm, ready to fly away. "And?" she asked.

"Why, nutritious, of course! Stormy, they tell me that one Sultana has more vitamins than a dozen oranges!"

"They do sound good," she said. "I'd like to try one of those, someday. A firm, sweet, juicy cloud . . ."

"Well," said Gnat. "Very nice. Goosebeak is returning to base."

Nimble and Prestor agreed. The three climbed behind the controls of their helicopters, rotors began to whirl.

"I'll stay awhile," said Baxter. "Stormy might need some help."

Prestor smiled. "She's had all the help she can refuse, tonight. She's flying south, he's flying north, Baxter, but those two are going to be lost in each other all the way home. Stormy's not likely to be an eager listener."

"No matter," said the newest fairy. "I'll fly along with her, anyway."

Stormy glanced out the rain-streaked window into dark. The weather has moved through Redding, soon it will be off the airway, too. She'd give it another few minutes.

"So what do you fly now, Strobe?"

He shrugged. "Gliders. And I've got a little biplane."

At once he became more attractive to her. Gliders? He flies for fun! She widened her eyes, watched him closely. "Oh? And what sort of a biplane?"

The three angel ferret fairies lifted into the air. Baxter remained on the tabletop in front of his machine, watching Stormy, listening to the conversation.

"It's an Ag-Kit," said Strobe.

"You're an ag-pilot, are you? Seeds and plant food, flying under the telephone wires?"

“No. That’s like freight-dogging. I did my share of that, down South, till I ran out of courage. Again.” He took a sip of chocolate. “I found an old Ag-Kit and converted it to a two-seater. I fly youngsters in it, as much as I can. Their first rides. You can’t imagine the sight of those little faces . . . they don’t know you’re watching them, from the rear cockpit. They look around in the air like they’ve all of a sudden gone to heaven.” At once he thought he had said too much, rearranged his cup and plate. “I enjoy it.”

“Let me get this straight,” said Stormy. “You removed the seed hopper and you installed a front cockpit in an Ag-Kit biplane, and you take kits up for rides? That’s what makes you happy?”

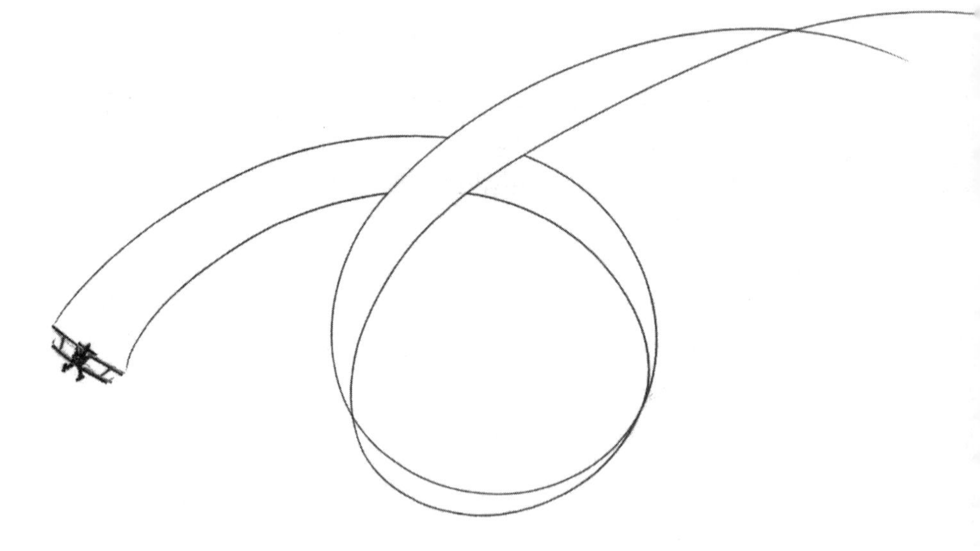

"Don't knock it till you try it, ma'am." How can she not like taking kits for rides? "Some of them, you change their lives! They go on, a few, they learn to fly . . ."

She reached her paw toward his, did not touch. "Strobe, I do the same thing in my seaplane. We're a boat for a while, taxiing on the water, then I let the kits push the throttle forward and away we go into the sky! That's a thrill, they like that."

He cleared his throat. "Well, what do you know . . ." Can it be? She flies because she loves flying, she shares flight with kits, and on top of it all she's so . . . incredibly . . . beautiful?

"I'm pleased to meet you, Strobe."

The way she said that, a hidden door opened to him, swept every possible reply from his mind.

Stormy changed her tone, yet left that inner door open. "And what brings you to Redding at this hour? You're not flying the Ag-Kit in the dark?"

"No," he said, recovering. Her paw had nearly touched his own. "I'm flying a different airplane tonight."

"Oh?"

He pointed out the window.

Gleaming under the ramp lights stood the FerrJet. It was the only aircraft in sight.

"Oh, my," she said. There fell a silence. "You're MusTel Two-Zero."

Stormy wanted to sink into the floor. How could she have been such a fool? *You fly, do you?* she had asked, of a corporate jet pilot who had more logbooks, probably, than she had hours in the air.

He nodded. "Thanks for the warning about the weather, Stormy."

"'*You fly, do you?*'" she said. "I'm so sorry, Strobe . . ."

"For nothing. The hat is not one that Stilton Ferret recommends for his pilots."

"But the FerrJet . . . you fly over the weather! What were you doing down with us freighters in the storm?"

He shrugged. "Strange thing. I had to fly low. Los Angeles to Medford, the cabin pressure failed just after takeoff. It's the outflow valve stuck open, I'm sure, an easy fix. But the oxygen tank was nearly empty, and without the pressure, of course . . ."

"You couldn't go high." She looked at him, bemused by events. We wouldn't have met.

He smiled at her. "Isn't that odd? If it weren't for an outflow valve and a Sacramento storm hotter than West Pittsburgh, you wouldn't be buying my pickles!"

She lifted her snow water, a toast to him. "If it weren't for your storm, and a bump or two over the Siskiyou, you wouldn't be treating me to breakfast. How I love coincidence. Healthy ferret food at no cost to myself!"

A bump or two? thought Baxter. *A bump or two?*

Strobe didn't raise his voice. "May?" he said. "You wouldn't have a Sultana pear for us, would you?"

She replied from the kitchen pass-through, her nose and whiskers appearing where they were not seen before. "They'll be on the menu when I go upscale, Captain Strobe. May's Airport Diners are for your starving pilots, they're for your good, wholesome airport food without the frills."

"Don't you deserve a frill, May? If I could arrange a box of Sultanas . . . ?"

"You just got your vittles free, kit! And your guest's, as well."

"Thanks, May," he said.

"Thank you, May," said Stormy, and then softly, "Thank you, Strobe."

He could barely speak. "My pleasure," he managed after a while. "So . . . how did you start to fly, Stormy?" He needed to know.

She watched him, considered the lightest of answers—I was unsafe on the ground—decided no.

"I had dreams when I was a kit," she told him. "I stood at the top of a big grassy hillside, then I'd run fast as I could, put my paws into the wind and I flew. It was beautiful, Strobe, looking down at the meadows below, the flowers."

He closed his eyes. "When you learned to fly, you were disappointed, weren't you? Wished you didn't need the airplane because the cockpit was so . . . mechanical . . ."

"Yes! Until after a thousand hours, the mechanical, it . . ." She reached for words. How can I tell him?

"It melts away."

She looked up at him. "It melts away."

"And there you are in the air."

"You dreamed it, too, didn't you? When you were a kit. The hillside?"

He nodded. He had never told anyone. "I've been looking for it ever since. I'd run down the slope . . ."

She turned away, looked out the window. ". . . and you'd fly . . ."

Then it was quiet, a silence gone as deep and comfortable as though all at once they were old friends.

She spoke at last. "I'm glad we met, Strobe."

He nodded.

Outside, the rain had stopped.

Stormy caught her breath. The time!

"I'd better run." She reached for her scarf and cap. "I need to file a flight plan, be on my way. You know the weather at Salinas—fog by sunrise."

"The ferret food," said Strobe.

She smiled, rising. "It's good for you."

"Bell-balls in heavy weather. Sounds like Santa Ferret's on his way?"

She looked down to him, amused. "Now how would you know that?"

"Allentown to Pittsburgh."

She laughed, wanted to hug her new friend, hold him fast, tell him he was the only one she had ever met . . . She offered her paw instead. "A pleasure to meet you, Captain Strobe. I hope we meet again."

"In better weather." He stood, took her paw in his own, held it longer than ferret custom required.

The two thanked May once again, called good-byes to her, walked together from the diner, Baxter's helicopter darting out the door an instant before it shut. Overhead, the clouds parted, stars peeking down.

May's voice from behind them: "Captain Strobe! Your hat!"

He turned back, retrieved the rag and set it on his head, not bothering to smooth the earflaps into place. They walked in silence, stopped at the FerrJet. "Do you have a minute?" he asked. "Take a look at the flight deck?"

"I'd love to see it sometime. I need to run, now."

"Good-bye, Stormy."

She set off to the Air Ferrets hangar, in a moment turned to him, walking backward, laughing. "Captain Strobe, your hat! Unforgettable!"

He smoothed the ragged flaps down over his ears, knew that wouldn't help. "Then don't forget, Janine! Have a good flight . . ."

She waved her paw, disappeared toward the hangar. He watched well after she was gone.

She takes kits for rides. In her seaplane.

He stood in the cold dark.

Whom, have I, just met?

CHAPTER 6

THE ANTENNA was replaced, the spark plugs changed on the number four engine.

"It ground-checks okay," Bella told the pilot, "but with your permission, Captain, I'd like to look at the magnetos. Could be something worse, you know. Could be a cam ring . . ."

"Gotta get my wheels up, Bella. I'm sure it'll run fine."

"Well, you've got three other big fans out there to keep you cool," the mechanic replied cheerfully. "Oh, Stormy. Speaking of . . . What's the difference between an albino ferret and a ceiling fan?"

On takeoff, not a hundred paws in the air, the number four engine backfired, once, a shower of sparks streaming into the night. Stormy shot a glance to her right, checked the temperatures and pressures shortly before the SkyFreighter was swallowed into the weather.

Refreshed from her stop at Redding, though, she agreed with the mechanic. If she had to shut an engine down, there were three others to fly on. And it was not so far to Salinas.

A ceiling fan turns clockwise. She smiled, in such a glad place of heart that she would have seen Baxter flying at her wingtip, had she turned to look.

Before dawn she was almost to Salinas, tired as a badger, refreshment worn away, flying by paw through the last of the storm.

"Air Ferret Three-Five, this is Monterey Approach Control, we have you in radar contact. Fly heading two-six-zero for vectors to the Salinas one-zero-seven degree radial. Confirm you have Information Bravo."

The recorded weather still echoed in her headset. "Salinas Airport Information Bravo for ferret aircraft: wind calm, indefinite ceiling overcast at two hundred paws, altimeter two-nine-zero-five, Runway Three-One visual range one thousand eight hundred paws."

This ought to be interesting, thought Baxter, flying close enough now to watch the pilot through her flight deck window. I've never seen an approach to minimums.

"We have Bravo," said Stormy. "We're level at five thousand five."

"Ferret Three-Five, you're cleared for the Salinas ILS Runway Three-One approach, maintain five thousand five hundred paws, present heading to the Salinas one-zero-seven degree radial, heading one-nine-seven degrees to intercept the localizer, contact Salinas tower at the marker."

Stormy suspected that Monterey Approach was betting she'd call again soon, flying her missed approach, diverting to an alternate airport.

That will not happen. The image flashed through her mind: an innocent kit reaching for toast and pickles, instead of proper ferret food this morning. If Salinas has bare minimum visibility, she vowed, we *will* be landing. Then she smiled. Toast and pickles.

At that moment the number four engine coughed, and again. Then it blew up.

As the pilot turned, startled, sparks burst to flame pouring from the cowling, a giant torch directly upon the wing, a fraction of a paw from the SkyFreighter's fuel tank. The fourth fire-suppression handle overhead illuminated, flashing white and red, alarm bell raucous on the flight deck.

With neither word nor change of expression, Stormy Ferret pulled the number four engine fuel selector to *Off,* its propeller lever to *Feather,* tugged its fire-suppression handle, slapped its mixture lever to *Idle-Cutoff,* its magneto switch *Off.*

Flames disappeared in a dense cloud of scarlet powders from the fire bottle, the exploding sounds fell away into the smooth drone of cruise flight, quieter than before, the number four propeller blades slowing, stopping at last, edges to the wind, stark and still in the glare of the right-side ice-light. Black oil streamed from the number four cowling, blown in the wind.

Airspeed sighed away, and the pilot increased the power on the remaining engines to keep her transport in the sky.

Stormy shook her head. Almost made it, she thought, not quite. She took no notice that she was trembling. No time for fear in the air when action's required, she had learned, no need for fear when the action's over.

Outside, Baxter's helicopter darted to the failed engine. Connecting rods had broken inside, he couldn't tell how many, pushing pistons through the top of cylinders, nearly through the engine cowling.

He was spun in dismay. Why was this happening? He had ordered no such failure. Stormy had met her destiny, she had diverted to Redding and found Strobe when otherwise they would have missed. She did not need another test before sunrise.

Stormy turned the SkyFreighter to the new heading, wheeled into a soft right bank as her transport found the final approach course. Then she cleared her mind and forgot all goals but one: tonight she must fly the perfect instrument approach.

Soon she watched the glide-slope needle ease down from the top of the navigation display to the center, held the centerline smoothly. Not long after, blue light flashed on the panel: the Salinas outer marker. She touched her approach timer to *Start,* checked her altitude against the number on the approach plate, set the flap handle to one-third down, moved the landing gear handle down.

Nothing happened, an empty click from the handle. Of course, she thought. The number four engine drove the aircraft hydraulic pump. No engine, no hydraulic pressure. She would have to pump the wheels down by paw, on the standby system.

The first approach had better be the good one, she thought. Once lowered by the emergency system, the wheels could not be retracted.

She moved the landing gear hydraulic selector to *Standby,* extended the emergency hydraulic handle and pumped it swiftly with her right paw, holding course and altitude down on the instrument landing system with her left.

After seventy pumps the uplocks released and the landing gear swung down. Swift air rumbled below, whirlwinds pouring around the gear doors as they opened, wheels lowering ponderously, one after another, thumping to lock in place.

"Salinas Tower," she panted, "Ferret Three-Five is the marker inbound on the ILS."

Three green lights glowed to her right. Landing gear is down and locked, she thought, too exhausted to say it aloud.

The captain knew that she should declare an emergency. If she did, the control tower would launch the fire engines, rush special handling for an Air Ferrets airplane.

I do not require special handling, she declared, I can take care of myself.

It was a mistake that she did not tell the tower her airplane was in trouble. If she failed the approach, if she crashed now, she would crash alone in the dark.

With a full load of cargo on board, flying on three engines, landing gear down, flaps down, the SkyFreighter was unable to climb. There would be no missed approach. Stormy's flight hung by the last link of its chain.

"Air Ferret Three-Five, this is Salinas Tower, you are cleared to land. Runway visual range is down to nine hundred paws."

Nine hundred paws was minimum legal visibility for ferret aircraft.

Stormy clicked her microphone button to acknowledge, advanced the power on three engines to hold her descent at five hundred paws per minute. The glide path fell away beneath her, faster than she had expected. She thought of the terrain in the fog below, mountains crowding both sides of her approach.

Stay on that glide path, Stormy, stay on the centerline!

She pulled the throttles back, farther than necessary with a failed engine, and the SkyFreighter sank down to meet the glide path. Power up to hold it.

Baxter was helpless, save to offer a blanket of confidence. "You're a professional pilot, Stormy. You've done this a thousand times before. You can shoot this approach. Piece of cake."

"Five hundred paws above minimums," she said aloud to her flight deck, feeling better without knowing why. "Wheels are down and locked."

Her life was in her paws, in her own skill, a perfect final approach. For the first time in her career, she had to land whether she could see the runway or not.

Landing lights on, a sheet of white, solid fog outside, a hundred paws above minimums.

Fifty paws.

"Good, Stormy," said Baxter. "You're doing fine. You chose this life, you practiced for it. You're a great airplane pilot."

Good, Stormy, she told herself, holding the ILS needles nearly centered, nearly a perfect cross on her instrument panel. On centerline, just above glide path . . . She breathed evenly now, a little pressure back on the wheel to center the needle of the glide slope. Though her heart was racing, her spirit was one with her airplane, smoothly together, easing down, reaching for the earth.

Baxter knew the instant it happened; he sensed it. The Salinas airport had gone to fog, ceiling zero visibility zero. Somehow, he had to open a tunnel in the cloud, let Stormy see to land. She has to see!

The world of mortals is a world of imagination, he had learned, and it changes by thought. He imagined the runway clear, bright moonlight, fog suddenly gone.

Stormy glanced at the altimeter. A white light flashed dit-dit-dit-dit on her instrument panel—the middle marker, her minimum legal altitude, 279 paws above the ground. No runway in sight, said the rules, you must go around and try again or divert to a different airport. Her eyes left the instruments for an instant, quick glance to the windshield. Solid fog. No runway.

Good, Stormy, she thought, fly it smooth, fly it so smooth . . .

On centerline, a little high on glide path . . . She eased the throttles back, visualized her wheels gentling down.

That instant, a hundred paws in the air, there came a sudden flicker in the mist, a flash of green threshold lights, black runway and giant white numbers, *31,* thrown against the dark and gone, glare from her landing lights in fog.

"Moonlight, moonlight," Baxter muttered. "No fog. Bright, clear air . . ." Nothing happened.

The ferret brought her three throttles gently back while she sat tall in her seat, looking out the windshield, hoping for a single runway stripe to flash toward her from the fog as the nose of the freighter rose, tires just a few paws above what she hoped was pavement.

So glad I didn't declare the emergency, she thought, for the chance I'd hit a fire truck, in the fog. The glass might as well have been snow, and her eyes flew back to the instrument panel.

"Heading-heading-heading!" she scolded. "Hold that compass straight on, Captain, dead-on, no matter what! Heading, heading!"

Came the chirp of rubber touching pavement, the transport wreathed in mist, runway invisible. The second her nosewheel touched down, the pilot pulled propellers two and three into reverse pitch, steered her heading not a single degree left or right, pressed hard on the SkyFreighter's brake pedals.

Stormy was all tense agony, waiting for the rumble and crash as her plane rolled high-speed off the runway into whatever waited in the dark.

The crash never came. In one long moment, the transport slowed to stop on the Salinas runway, she had not a clue where. From her cockpit, window slid open, engines idling, she could not see the ground.

His helicopter a few paws from Stormy's window, Baxter's eyes were nearly closed, concentrating. "Clear skies, clear tunnel of air opening before us . . ."

It happened. From ground to a hundred paws in the air, the fog disappeared. Stormy saw wet runway shining under her landing lights, a taxiway not a hundred paws ahead. She pressed the throttles of her inboard engines forward, and the SkyFreighter began to move.

"Ferret Three-Five's clear the runway," she called, "taxi Air Ferrets terminal."

The tower controller could not have seen her landing in the fog. If no one said anything about arriving below minimums, it would all be legal and forgotten.

"Ferret Three-Five, remain this frequency, taxi to the terminal. Did you notice the ceiling when you broke out?"

"Three-Five, sorry I didn't," she said. "How are you doing this morning?"

"We were in solid fog till a second ago. Patchy stuff. It must be better on the runway."

Baxter floated in triumph, hovering above the transport. He had cleared the fog!

The next second, however, the cloud fell as though its strings had been cut. In fluffy darkness, the pilot struggled to hold the secret blue glow from the nearest taxiway marker.

Safe on the ground, the ferret captain went limp with fatigue, caught herself at once.

"Hang on, Stormy," she said aloud. "This flight is not over untill you are parked at the terminal. Just a little more, and it's easy . . ."

35

Taxiing through night fog from one isolated blue light to another, trusting experience to stay on an invisible taxiway is not so easy as her confident words, but no longer did her cargo and her life hang in the balance.

Finally, groping through the dark, the mist thinned and she recognized a vague outline, the Air Ferrets terminal.

The ground-crew ferret saw her, waved two lighted wands, guiding the SkyFreighter that loomed from the cloud to its place by the loading dock.

Hi, Travis, she thought. Earnest and hardworking, the young animal had told her about his flight lessons, promised that one day he would be a cargo pilot, too.

At last he crossed the wands overhead in his paws, *X* for "stop." Then, happy for Stormy's arrival, he saluted her smartly.

The pilot smiled, set the brakes, touched the bill of her cap in response.

She finished her after-landing checklist, brought the mixture levers of the three remaining engines to *Idle-Cutoff,* thanking them for the power they had given, listened to their low thunder suddenly vanished into the silence of a predawn airport. Cool air washed from the side window onto the flight deck.

"On time!" Travis called up to her.

"Almost," she replied, the word sounding harsh and strange in the quiet.

As she shut down radios and master switch, she heard the ground crew clattering a stairway to the side of the transport, the whine of the main entrance door sliding upward.

"Thank you, all my guardian angels tonight," she said aloud. "I needed you."

Hovering over the ruined engine, Baxter did not catch her comment.

Now Stormy returned her charts and approach plates to her flight bag, reached for the aircraft maintenance log.

Autopilot tugs to right on engaging, then circuit breaker fails system, she wrote in neat, clear letters. *De-icing system overloads with continued use, then circuit breaker fails system when power applied. Multiple lightning strikes. Numerous instrument lights broken in turbulence. Number four engine severe vibration, flame from cowling. Fire suppression activated, engine shut down in flight. Landing gear extended by emergency system.*

She wrote this without distress. Most often the Air Ferrets SkyFreighters were trouble-free. Once in a while, of course, every pilot has her tests.

Loadmaster Max Ferret was first through the entrance door. He turned aft, opened the side cargo doors for the unloading crew, then came forward to stand in the space behind the center console on the flight deck, gave the pilot a long look.

"We had a problem with our number four engine?"

Stormy nodded. "Hi, Max. Just a little." She listened to the whine of a forklift, hoisting the first of the ferret-food containers from the hold. "We may need a new cylinder out there."

"May need," said Max. "May need several. You had to pump the wheels down, I guess?"

She nodded again.

"Weather's a bit low," he said. "We were surprised you made it."

She nodded a third time. "Piece of cake," she added, then smiled. "Too much cake, though, is not good for ferrets."

Finishing her logbook entry, she looked up at him. "Three of the containers broke loose, Max. I tied them back the best I could. Is the cargo safe?"

He touched her shoulder, kidded her gently. "The ferrets in Salinas, Stormy, every one, shall have their proper food this week."

"Not toast and pickles?" she said, a tired smile for her friend.

He looked out the right side-window at the number four engine, blackened from the fire, dripping oil. "Nice job, Captain. Nice job of flying."

She shrugged. "Cargo for Seattle?"

"Portland–Seattle–Coeur d'Alene. Tomorrow midnight."

"Airway Victor Two-Three," she said. "I'll fly it."

She unstrapped her shoulder harness, rose from her seat, stretched luxuriously, then lifted her flight bag and walked to the entrance-door stairway, dawn fog swirling into the airplane.

At the foot of the stairs, waiting patiently, stood a distinguished-looking ferret in a devastated corduroy hat. In his paw a scarlet box, tied with ribbons.

"Hi, Stormy."

"Strobe!"

"Have a good flight?"

She ran down the steps to him, fatigue vanished. "Strobe! How did you . . . ?"

He said nothing.

She looked about, saw the FerrJet parked in the mist near the Air Ferrets terminal.

"Oh. You beat me here. How was your approach?"

"Easy," he said. "Ceiling was five hundred paws when I landed."

"Good."

Strobe watched her. "It was lower for you."

"A bit." She looked up at him, her silver fur and dark eyes the picture of adventures past and yet to come.

"I'd like to hear about that," he said, offering the scarlet box.

She sniffed the wrappings. "Could this be a firm, sweet, juicy cloud?"

"Let's find out."

They walked together toward the terminal.

"Did you say you take *kits* up in your seaplane?" he asked. "All those little paws touching the controls? Why would you do a thing like that?"

The two disappeared toward the terminal, lost in each other, leaving Baxter to hover in the dawn.

Helmet and goggles, Stormy had told him. He couldn't send Willow any but spiritual gifts, yet somehow, there had to be a way to let her know . . .

The angel ferret fairy tilted his helicopter forward, accelerating, climbing like a homesick angel ferret fairy, high into the sky.

CHAPTER 7

THE CLOUD was a giant cavern in the air, lit within, a maintenance bay for angel ferret fairy helicopters parked in rows, each to its own numbered spot.

Baxter landed on 35, stepped out to the sound of mechanics' air drills, rivet guns, socket wrenches turning.

The old-timers here knew none of it was necessary, that the helicopters could be maintained by thought alone, that fairies can fly without machines if they wish, yet pilots and mechanics so loved messing with aircraft, as they had when they were mortals, that no one questioned the custom.

"Welcome back," said Geoffrey, the helicopter mechanic, his nose smudged with engine oil. "You're way overdue."

"Sorry."

"No need for that. We haven't worried here for so long I'm afraid we've forgotten how to do it." He looked at the pilot carefully. "Tired?"

Baxter smiled at the joke. "I can be tired if I want to be, Geoff. It hasn't been that long, for me." He yawned, as much for nostalgia's sake as for demonstrating his words.

The mechanic climbed to the rotor hub, happily running the postflight inspection. "You've lost a safety wire here," he said. "You didn't let your rotor overspeed, did you?"

"I'm not sure. It was a rough flight. There was a lot happening."

"You took your rotor overspeed."

Geoffrey noted it so calmly that Baxter asked, "What's the harm?"

"None. Machines can't be hurt here any more than we can. But I'll replace the rotor."

"If there's no harm . . ."

The mechanic paused his inspection, whiskers askew against the rotor mast, glanced at the angel ferret fairy. "Do you like flying?"

"Of course I like flying. I love flying!"

"Loves don't leave us when we graduate from earth," Geoffrey said. He climbed down from the machine, lifted a pair of diagonal pliers, a socket wrench and a spanner from his toolbox. "You love flying helicopters, we love working on 'em."

They talked for a while as Geoffrey rested the golden blades carefully on rotor stands, clipped safety wire from the attach fittings, removed bolts and laid them carefully on a stand. "She's got a grand transmission," he said, and then in wonder to himself, "the clutch, inside, it's liquid ferret-metal . . ."

After a while Baxter made his way out of the hangar, toward the angel ferret fairy base exchange, thinking of Willow and Daphne.

Dying did not end Baxter's relationship with his mate. In time the two had learned, as had many ferret couples, that death is a doorway, not a wall. Each of them lifting above appearances, mortal and graduate both kept imagination open to messages from the other, trusting that what they imagined was true.

At first it had felt to Daphne as though she were inventing Baxter's voice, making up his messages in her mind. With practice, and with information she couldn't have imagined, she put doubts away.

Ungrieving, then, Daphne had been nearly as excited as Baxter by his choice to become an angel ferret fairy. Already she knew of his mission aloft with Stormy and Strobe; she yearned to hear the outcome.

Sitting relaxed, she found, eyes closed, fur unruffled, she could link her heart with Baxter's. In time it was easy.

She had told him that their eldest grandkit, Budgeron, successful now as a waiter in Manhattan, had begun writing stories. In return she marveled at Baxter's news that Willow, their youngest, would one day become a Teacher.

Little Willow, however, was not so immune as Daphne from distress at her grampa's dying.

The two had been inseparable, his grandkit riding on Baxter's lap while he flew his gyrocopter every sunny day from the field behind her home.

Death is not a wall, Baxter had learned, but grief is. He had been unable to get a single message through to the heartbroken little ferret except in dreams, now and then. Dreams forgotten. How he missed the touch of her bright spirit!

Down the corridors of the base exchange he walked, looking for toys that Willow might treasure. He lingered over a small box of spiritual understanding, decided it might be too grown-up a gift for her, just now.

A stand of colored bottles caught his eye: increased psychic powers. She already has all the psychic powers she needs, he thought. Too many bottles of psychic without that box of understanding, it's a curse, not a blessing.

As he was about to leave, he saw on a counter directly in front of him, a jar of simple cream, clear as air: the ability to see what already exists.

A thrill went through him. Perfect! He caught it up, bought it at once, rushed back to the quarters he had built from thought, a small thatched house on a hill above the river.

Baxter loved the sky, but he loved his little house, too. The view down the deep-grass slope to the meadows below, and the river, one might as well be flying.

He threw himself upon the hammock, closed his eyes, brought a picture of Daphne before his mind. Delicious. All heaven about him, yet to be with his mate as well!

"I knew it was you," she said in her imagination. "I was just about to call."

They talked for a while about the affairs of both worlds. He shared his adventure in the storms, every detail, his lesson from Geoffrey as well, the way our loves remain, one life to the next. In turn she told him of their kits and grandkits, said she was giving special attention to Willow, grieving for her grampa.

"I found a little gift for her," Baxter said, told Daphne of the jar and cream, the way it might let Willow see what was already there, might be a way to cheer her.

The spiritual gift could get through to Daphne easily enough, they decided, wrapped in love. "But how," he asked, "can we get it from you to Willow?"

There was a silence, each of them light as clouds, touching hearts.

"It's a cream?"

"Sort of a cream. Like soft, smooth air."

After a moment of reflection: "Why, Bax, that's simple! I'll spread it over something of yours, rub it in, then just hand it to her, let her play!"

"Something of mine?"

"One of your old scarves, she'd love that, or a hat, there's plenty of those . . ."

In a flash, he knew. "Not a hat, Daph. My helmet and goggles! They're on the peg by the door in the garage. Give her my fluffy old flying helmet and goggles!"

"It's got airplane oil on it. Remember the day you were changing the oil in the gyrocopter and Willow asked, 'Grampa, why are you wearing your helmet and goggles to change the oil?'"

He laughed. "All the better! To remember that day, it'll help set her free. Through the goggles, she'll see what's real. Happiness for sorrow, joy for grief. Maybe even her grampa in his helicopter, right there in front of her. I'm tired of her looking through me when I'm with her, Daph, when I'm practically landing on her nose!"

Thus the mystical jar was passed from Baxter to his mate across the border of life in one form and life in another, the two conspiring that it should be soaked and rubbed by paw into the flier's old helmet and goggles and presented to his youngest grandkit.

The gift to see what already exists.

CHAPTER 8

THE SKY rolled beneath her. From the front seat of the open-cockpit Ag-Kit, Stormy turned to look back, caught Strobe's eyes watching hers.

Soft-fabric helmets and goggles they wore, and silken scarves whipping in the wind. When she rolled the little biplane inverted once again, she laughed and released the control stick, pressed the interphone button.

"You've got it, Strobe!"

Her joke to him, and a test. Would the owner roll his aircraft back to straight and level or pull the control stick back, split-S down and away? The first would lose no altitude, the second would lose a lot.

"Why, thank you, Stormy!" He spent less than a second to be startled that she would give him the controls while the 'Kit was upside down, held the pressures just as she had left them, added opposite rudder while the machine rolled, smoothly reversed it to bring them back to level flight.

Then Strobe pulled the nose to the noon sun. When the airspeed had fallen nearly to zero, he let go of the controls, Stormy's own medicine back to her. "It's all yours, beautiful!"

"What a mean ferret!" She laughed, taking the stick in her paws, touching it gently forward, pressing full rudder. The plane pivoted weightless, stopped in the air, its nose swiveling slowly to point from straight up to straight down.

Stormy pulled the throttle back, lifted the nose again when speed had returned and rolled the 'Kit once more. "I love your biplane, Captain!"

As they had shared an afternoon flying her seaplane from the sun-blue lake by her home, so they spent an afternoon here together, in the sky with his biplane.

"I have to go, Stormy," he told her after they had landed, the metal of the Ag-Kit's engine ticking softly as it cooled in the hangar.

"Whither bound?" she said, her feelings to herself.

"Florida. I need to take the F-Triple-Seven down there, fly Stilton from Orlando to Melbourne, then to St. Petersburg."

"He needs that huge airliner to fly Orlando–Melbourne–St. Pete? Strobe, he can do that in the helicopter. He can do it in his limousine!"

The pilot grinned. "Sorry," he said. "Stilton's flying from Orlando to Melbourne, Australia, then to St. Petersburg, Russia. The limo would be inconvenient."

Stormy ducked, laughing. "Well, excuse me!"

They were good friends now, Stormy and Strobe. They missed each other when they were apart.

CHAPTER 9

SINCE HER GRANDFATHER had died, Willow had worn her wolf hat, as though somehow the fierce thing might protect her from an uncaring world. A snarling gray-flannel wolf head it was, black buttons for eyes, mouth agape. And there inside was little Willow, gazing out, sadly, from behind the wooden fangs.

When Daphne came to visit that Saturday, Willow brightened, a rare sparkle in her eyes.

"Gra'ma!" she called when her father opened the door. She held out her paws to be picked up.

Daphne touched hello to her son Raja, a gentle stroke at the side of his neck. She handed him a box to hold, its wrapping a cloud of helicopters, and swept beyond.

"There's my Willow-tree!"

She scooped her grandkit from the carpet, swung her through the air in a circle, their noses and whiskers nearly touching. Baxter had whirled her so, every visit, and the little one would squeal with glee.

When the turns were finished, Willow nestled on her grandmother's shoulder.

"Where's Grampa?"

"Grampa's with you."

"Grampa?" The kit looked for him, wolf hat turning left and right. She didn't find him, and the sparkle left her eyes.

What a bond, Daphne thought, between those two. She sensed the presence of her mate, felt his excitement at what was to come.

"Willow," she said. "Grampa sent you a present."

The wolf hat turned suddenly toward Daphne, as did Raja, and from the kitchen beyond, his mate, Skye.

"Raj . . ." said Daphne.

Willow's father brought the package, gay-ribboned, set it on the carpet in front of his kit. Her eyes looked to them both, and to her mother. Then she turned and looked behind. Grampa might be hiding.

For a moment she paused, almost as if she sensed the salt-and-pepper of her grandfather's mask, saw his wink to her: Go ahead, Willow, open it! She turned back to the gift.

Holding the box between her paws, she untied the bows, carefully unfolded the paper, raised the lid. Pulling aside the tissue within, she froze, looked to Daphne. Then, delicately, Willow reached inside and lifted the rich old fabric of Baxter's flying helmet, oil-stained, goggles dangling from their strap.

"Grampa . . ." So softly she whispered that no one heard.

She swept the wolf hat from her head, let it fall to the floor.

Refusing help, Willow slipped the helmet about her head and ears, set the goggles on her forehead at the same jaunty angle that Baxter once did, landing his gyrocopter in the meadow.

"Thank you, Gra'ma!"

Then Willow reached up and lowered the goggles over her eyes.

Her jaw dropped. "Oh . . ."

At once her face wreathed in smiles. *"Dook-dook!"* she said. "Grampa! *Dook-dook-dook!"*

She leaped up, spread her paws like wings, dashed about the room light as a kitten chasing string. This way she darted, this way and that, dooking for all the world as though she had changed from ferret kit to baby helicopter.

Skye came to stand with Raja and his mother, astonished at what she saw. For so long Willow had been wasting away, drawing back, drawing back. All of a sudden, this.

For Willow, it was no miracle. Grampa couldn't leave her, he loved her too much to leave her, she knew he did. If only she called enough for him, inside, he'd come back.

When she lowered the goggles over her eyes, there he was. There his dear, funny face, merry eyes, mask and whiskers unchanged, Grampa sitting in a shining golden helicopter, rotors turning *dook-dook*.

"Willow!" he called, patting the seat beside him. *"Come fly, Willow!"*

She ran, sprang through door, threw her arms around his neck. *"Grampa!* You're back!"

"Silly kit," he told her. "I was never gone! I was with you, I'm with you now!"

"I didn't see . . ."

He frowned playfully. "Oh, you didn't see. But what did your heart say?"

"Grampa loves me! He'd never leave!"

"Your heart knows, Willow, *your heart knows!"*

Then off the ground they lifted, bright rotors tilting forward, *dook-dook-dook,* zooming ahead, over the couch, blurring by the bookshelves, by the family picture, all the ferrets together, Willow on Grampa's knee.

Baxter climbed the bright machine straight up, hovered backward, flew sideways, stopped midair to watch Mom and Dad and Gra'ma, tears in their eyes for no reason.

"So much to learn, Willow-tree!"

"Of course, Grampa. I came to teach."

Baxter turned to stare at her, the helicopter nearly colliding with a floor lamp.

"You *know?*"

Watching her kit, Skye reached for Daphne, hugged her as though she would never let her go.

Raja stared at the scene. "Mom, how did you . . . ?"

"Your father thought it might be worth a try. He found it in the angels' store."

Watching Willow come to life, no one found that strange.

The kit slowed her mad flyings, hovered to a stop, staring through the goggles into empty air. Then she turned slowly, till her eyes came to rest upon the grown-ups, watching her. It was as though Willow saw lights of silver and gold about her elders, as though she understood, as though the impossible had become simple.

She lifted the goggles, same easy twist of her paw. "Thank you," she said. "Thank you, Dad and Mom, thank you, Gra'ma. Thank you, Grampa."

You're welcome, they mouthed silently.

Willow nodded. "I'm a Teacher," she said, that little voice. "Can I be a Teacher, Mom?"

There was silence in the room.

"Of course you can be a Teacher, my Willow," said Skye. "If you're chosen, if you love enough, and learn . . ."

"I'm a Teacher."

The kit set off for her room, goggles perched above her eyes. She left the wolf hat on the floor, and never did she wear it again.

CHAPTER 10

FROM HIS OFFICE high above Manhattan, at the top of the MusTelCo building, the world's richest ferret tilted in his chair, swiveled it a slow half-turn to look out upon the city.

"You've never asked for anything," he said, a hidden smile for his friend. "As long as we've known each other, Strobe, you've never asked for anything."

The pilot sat opposite, watched the same view. He could see the tips of Stilton's ears over the back of the chair, turned away. "Not true. I ask all the time. I ask for the best airplanes, the best pilots, the best mechanics . . ."

"That's not asking, that's your job. Your life and mine, the life of every ferret who steps aboard a MusTelCo aircraft, we're in your paws. I expect the best."

Stilton turned again, swiveled slowly to face the flier.

Strobe held his gaze. "I'm asking now. The world needs pilots because it needs flight. Kits deserve perspective, and they get that when they fly. The deserve to learn how to command themselves! The biplanes are a long-term investment, Stilton."

"'*Kits for Kits.*" The chairman of the board and chief executive officer lifted a pen, jotted the line on a letterhead notepad. "You propose, all around the country, centers where kits can come, they rebuild old ag-planes, they learn to fly. You encourage other companies to support these centers. And this pays off for us . . . how?"

Strobe smiled. So many times he had heard the question.

"It's the second line, Stilton, that pays off for us: *Kits for Kits—a MusTelCo Flight Center.* MusTelCo's investing in all those kits who love the sky, investing in the future of us all. MusTelCo's bringing the romance of flight to kits who otherwise . . . MusTelCo equals Romance, Stilton! MusTelCo equals Adventure!"

"And that'll make you happy?"

"No. I'm already happy." Strobe touched his scarf, midnight striped in gold. "I'm asking because it's my highest right, and because it's terrific for the company—not for us to say we're the spirit of the future, but for us to show it!"

Those dark eyes, that mask familiar to ferrets around the world, Stilton watched his friend. "Tell me what Stormy thinks about your plan."

The chief pilot grinned at his boss. "It's her idea. She'll never admit it. 'It's not the one who has the idea that matters—it's the one who makes it happen!'"

The chairman placed the pen softly back in its holder. For so long, they had been friends. Since college, when Strobe left school to begin his life in the air. All this time each had remained without a mate, Strobe for his here-and-gone flying schedule, Stilton isolated at the peak of the glass mountain that was MusTelCo.

Now Strobe has found a mate, thought Stilton. At last. He closed his eyes, glad once again for his friend. How I wish I could do the same. I try to see her, imagine her, but everything's misty.

"Then it's done," said the CEO. "Let's go for the first hundred Ag-Kits. You show me the company's become adventure and romance and we'll buy every old crate you can find out there, build 'em back to train your kits. And don't forget the scarf, Strobe, it's part of the program."

Strobe raised a paw to brush the side of his nose. "If I might suggest . . ."

"I agree. No MusTelCo there. Raw silk. Pure white. Every kit who learns to fly. They'll keep it forever, we don't need the logo."

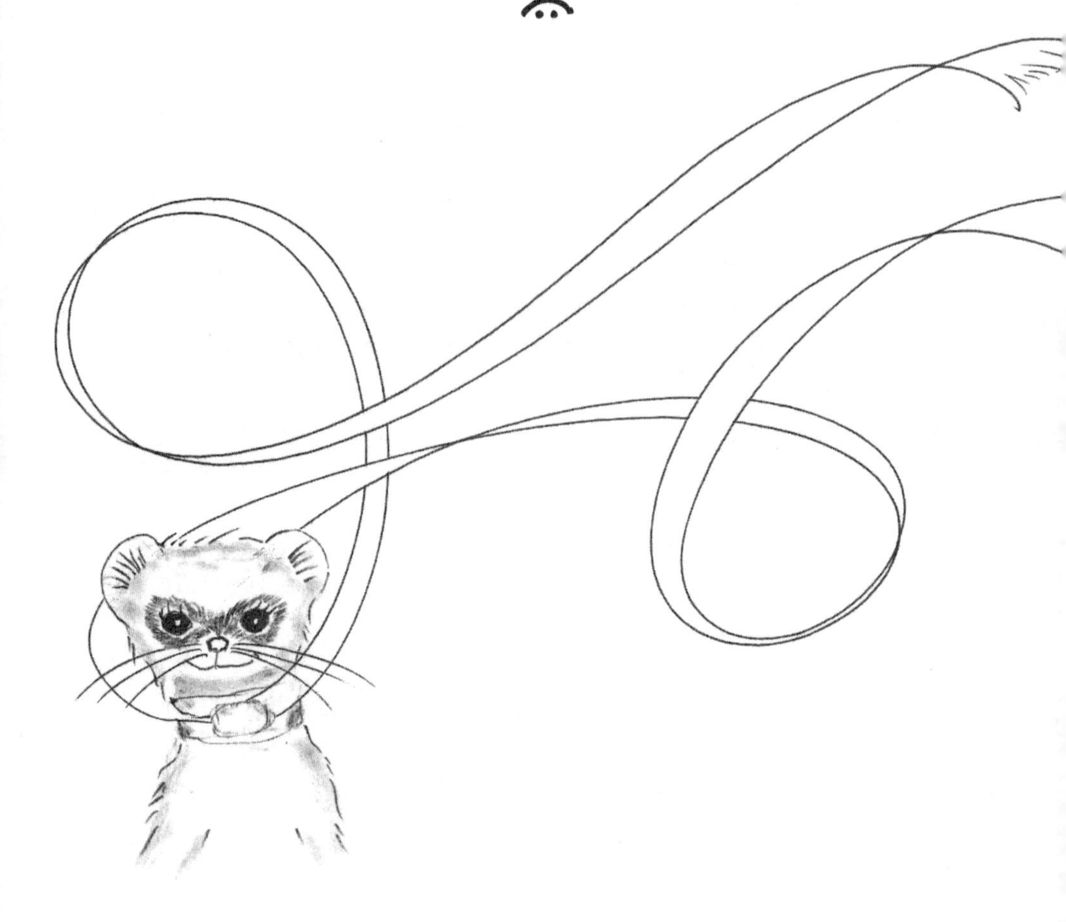

That's how it began. Stormy and Strobe brought together by the thoughtful courtesy of a tempest on the airways; crafty Stilton won over to adventure and romance.

Before long the sound of bright-color biplanes had returned to the air, kits coming home to the high blue land of the sky, noses and whiskers chilled in the dawn, scarves flying. They learned courage and daring and self-reliance, how to navigate among the clouds as well as among the challenges and tests of their lifetimes. They graduated resolved to meet their highest right, to share what they had found, to give back to others the gifts they had themselves been given.

The world changed, by the love of two who loved the sky. By the love of more, counting angel ferret fairies on a dimension just out of sight, arranging coincidence for mortals as they have since beyond remembering.

Once Stormy found Strobe, of course, in time she found young Willow, a Columbine like herself, and a Teacher.

The tale of how they met, and how the world was changed once again, that's another story.

Ferret House Press